"We need to acknowledge some things before we proceed," Daniel said, holding her gaze. "I want you."

Her lips parted on a sharp indrawn breath. Then Megan nodded with wide eyes, accepting his desire or admitting her own—he wasn't sure.

"But we can't act on this attraction. We can't add more lies to our deception."

"No, we can't," she said in a small voice, her guilt plain on her face. "We...we could be partners. Co-parenting partners. Nothing more."

"Agreed. We'll be partners."

They sat in silence for a while. When he glanced up, his eyes caught on her bottom lip, which she worried between her teeth. He swallowed and resolutely shifted his focus to her forehead.

As lovely as it was, it seemed safer than staring into her beautiful eyes, which were dangerously close to her plump, pink lips.

* * *

One Night Only by Jayci Lee
is part of the Hana Trio series.

Dear Reader,

I wrote *One Night Only* while my dad was in the hospital and edited it right after he passed away. As I was editing this book, I realized that I modeled much of Minsung Han, Megan's dad, after my own dad—especially his unconditional love for his daughters.

Of course the love story between Megan and Daniel is the heart of *One Night Only*, but the relationship between the heroine and her dad means so much to me. Without realizing it, I wrote it as a tribute to my dad and how much—how dearly—he loved me.

There is a scene in the story where Minsung Han says something poetic followed quickly by "I'm no poet." It makes me smile and think "Yes, you are" because my dad *was* a poet. It's like a little Easter egg I hid in the story for myself.

Working on this book held me together and saved me during one of the most heartbreaking times of my life. Writing is a talent my dad passed on to me. Every time I create these characters and stories to share with you, my reader, I will remember that my dad lives on through me.

I hope *One Night Only* warms your heart and brings you comfort and joy. It is truly a gift and an honor to have you as my reader. Thank you.

With love,

Jayci Lee

JAYCI LEE

———

ONE NIGHT ONLY

HARLEQUIN
DESIRE

HARLEQUIN®
DESIRE™

Recycling programs
for this product may
not exist in your area.

ISBN-13: 978-1-335-58158-7

One Night Only

Harlequin Enterprises ULC
22 Adelaide St. West, 41st Floor
Toronto, Ontario M5H 4E3, Canada
www.Harlequin.com

Printed in U.S.A.

Jayci Lee writes poignant, sexy and laugh-out-loud romance every free second she can scavenge. She lives in sunny California with her tall, dark and handsome husband, two amazing boys with boundless energy, and a fluffy rescue whose cuteness is a major distraction. At times, she cannot accommodate reality because her brain is full of drool-worthy heroes and badass heroines clamoring to come to life.

Because of all the books demanding to be written, Jayci writes full-time now and is semiretired from her fifteen-year career as a defense litigator. She loves food, wine and traveling, and, incidentally, so do her characters. Books have always helped her grow, dream and heal, and she hopes her books will do the same for you.

Books by Jayci Lee

Harlequin Desire

The Heirs of Hansol

Temporary Wife Temptation
Secret Crush Seduction
Off Limits Attraction

Hana Trio

A Song of Secrets
One Night Only

Visit her Author Profile page at Harlequin.com, or jaycilee.com, for more titles.

You can also find Jayci Lee on Facebook, along with other Harlequin Desire authors, at Facebook.com/harlequindesireauthors!

In memory of Jae W. Chon.

Prologue

When Megan Han and her sisters performed as the Hana Trio, the sound of her violin, Angie's cello and Chloe's viola came together as one—as *hana*—to create the music of their hearts. The thrill, joy and fulfillment Megan derived from being a part of the trio couldn't be matched. She was living her dream—a dream she shared with her sisters—and she wouldn't have it any other way.

But lately, she felt a restlessness stirring inside her. She didn't know what it meant to stand on her own. A part of her felt transparent, like she wasn't a fully realized person yet. Maybe that was why she had agreed to play rock violin at the Tipsy Dahlia, a seedy nightclub in Hollywood, on the same night the Hana Trio was performing in the Chamber Music Society's last concert of the season. The timing wasn't ideal, but no-name performers—she didn't mention she was part of the Hana Trio—couldn't be choosers.

The electric violin was a recent preoccupation of hers *plus* she wanted to know if she could move an audience without her sisters and the clout of the Hana Trio. She wouldn't necessarily call this a rebellion, since she could do whatever the hell she wanted with her free time, but it did feel like her little secret. Something that was hers alone. She wasn't entirely sure how she felt about that. Probably both excited and scared.

The burst of applause snapped her out of her reverie and returned her to the backstage of the concert hall. Megan clapped along with the audience from behind the curtains. The Chamber Orchestra had performed beautifully.

"I can't believe it's the final night of the season," Chloe said, shaking her head.

"I know. Concert season feels grueling sometimes, but I'm going to miss playing in front of a big audience." Angie sighed. "Nothing matches the energy of these concerts."

"Well, let's go out there and generate enough energy to carry us through the off-season." Megan smoothed her hand down her claret, floor-length dress. "It's showtime, ladies."

She and her sisters were met by resounding applause as they strode onto the stage. Megan put her hand on her chest and smiled at the audience, filled with gratitude. The Hana Trio had gained renown in the last couple of years, due in part to the piece they were performing tonight—the string trio Angie's husband, Joshua Shin, had composed for them. Since they premiered the work last season, it had become one of their signature pieces and a definite fan favorite.

Silence fell around them when they took their seats. Megan brought her violin under her chin and held her sisters' eyes. With a subtle nod, she lowered her bow to the strings, and the first dulcet strains of the string trio filled the auditorium.

The beauty of the piece pulled her under its spell and she swayed with the music, playing the violin with her whole body. Her sisters danced and moved on each side of her, melody and harmony spilling from their instruments. She always imagined that they looked like three lithe trees, waving in the wind—their movements unsynchronized but graceful.

The concert hall remained eerily quiet as the last notes echoed into silence. Then, as though snapped awake by a hypnotist, the entire audience jumped to their feet, clapping in a quick staccato. Megan and her sisters rose from their seats and bowed deeply. Once, then twice. Her heart pounded with adrenaline and euphoria as they walked off the stage.

"I'm so proud of you guys." Angie hugged Chloe, then Megan, balancing her cello with one hand.

"We're proud of you, too." Megan returned her older sister's one-armed hug, holding her violin to the side.

"Don't forget Joshua," her younger sister chimed in. "We should give him some credit for writing that masterpiece."

"Thank you, Chloe," Joshua said, walking up to them. "You three sounded magnificent."

He wrapped his arm around Angie's waist and dropped a kiss on her forehead with tender affection. Megan watched the exchange with a dreamy sigh. Her soul mate would find her someday. She just wished he would stop taking his sweet time about it.

"I know I can't top praise like that from the composer himself." Their dad joined them backstage, beaming with pride. "But you girls played beautifully. It almost takes away the sting of not having any of my daughters follow in my footsteps."

He hugged Megan and Chloe but hesitated in front of her older sister. With a soft smile, Angie wrapped her arms around his waist and embraced him. His eyes closed for a second as though he wanted to commit the moment to his memory. Angie and their dad had been estranged for over six years until they began mending their relationship last year.

"Ahbunim." Joshua bowed from his waist.

"It's good to see you, son." Their dad patted his back before waving over a couple who had been standing a little apart from the group. "Girls, you remember Mr. and Mrs. Werner."

"You three have grown into such lovely, talented women," Anne Werner said with a tremulous smile. "Your mom would've been so proud."

Their dad was the CEO of Jigu Corporation, a thriving electronic components company, and Anne was a member of the board of directors. She had also been a dear friend of their mom's, who'd passed away from breast cancer seven years ago.

"Thank you, Anne," Megan said, squeezing her tightly. Her sisters joined in for a group hug.

"I also wanted to introduce you to our new CFO—" their dad glanced around with a perplexed frown "—but he didn't make it to the concert. He probably got held up at work."

"Such disrespect." Anne snorted with uncharacteristic disdain. "Minsung, I told you that young man is too arrogant for his own good."

"You're mistaking confidence for arrogance," he said evenly. "He's going to take Jigu Corporation to the next level. You'll see."

"Now, Anne." Tim Werner put his hand on his wife's shoulder when she took a deep breath in preparation for a retort. "Don't you think you should save the business talk for another time? Tonight is about the Hana Trio and the Chamber Music Society."

"Well said, Tim." Their dad clasped his hands together. "We should go out and celebrate. All of us."

"I, um…" Megan took a quick glance at the clock. *Crap.* She had less than an hour to get dressed and make it to Hollywood for her rock violin debut. She yawned loudly. "I am *exhausted*. I'm going to turn in early."

"Then, I'll come home with you," their dad said, concern clouding his expression. Guilt twisted in her gut. She hated lying, even when it was harmless. She just wasn't ready to share her rock violin debut with anyone yet, especially since she might bomb and prove once and for all that she was nothing without her sisters.

"Don't be silly. You should go celebrate with them. We drove separately anyway. I'll see you tomorrow morning, Appa." Before anyone could respond, she picked up her dress and hurried away from her family and friends. "Have fun, guys. Bye. Good night."

Alone in the dressing room—while her fellow musicians lingered backstage celebrating the last concert of the season—she stepped out of her formal dress and tugged on a pair of tight, ripped jeans and a black bustier top. Holding a hair tie between her lips, she shook her tasteful curls out as though she had a spider crawling in her head and pulled her tousled hair into a high ponytail. Then she made quick work of applying some charcoal eye shadow and a deep purple lipstick.

Megan smiled at the stranger looking out at her from the mirror. This was too much fun. Not wanting to explain her attire to anyone, she slipped out of the dressing room and made a beeline for her car. By the time she started the engine and drove out to the street, she was down to forty-five minutes. She pushed her candy-red Carrera as fast as she dared, swerving in and out of lanes. She could almost hear her little sister lecturing her that driving like an asshole would only get her to her destination an average of three minutes faster.

Well, she needed every minute she could scavenge. She refused to be late for her first performance. She might have decided to perform on an impulsive whim, but she was a professional musician and she couldn't keep her audience waiting. But two blocks from the concert hall, her car slowed and sputtered. She barely had time to pull over to the curb before it died on her with a soft whine.

"No, no, no." She grabbed and shook the steering wheel as though she could wake her car up. When that didn't work, she stomped to the rear of the vehicle and popped the hood to take a look at the engine. She grabbed her forehead and cursed. "I don't even know what I'm supposed to check."

A black Maserati pulled out of traffic and parked behind her. *Thank heavens for Good Samaritans.* Curious who her rescuer might be, she craned her neck to watch as a man stepped out of the car—a tall, gorgeous man with black hair swept off his forehead, deep coffee-brown eyes and amazing cheekbones. She would literally kill for his bone structure.

Megan belatedly realized his distractingly scrumptious lips were moving. She gave her head a sharp shake and said, "I'm sorry. What was that?"

"Do you need some help?" he asked in a sexy baritone, coming to stand next to her.

"Yes, my car went belly-up." She stared at her engine again to stop herself from ogling the stranger.

"I can take a look." He unbuttoned his dress shirt at the wrist and rolled up his sleeve, revealing a superb forearm. "Do you want to try starting the engine?"

"Yeah. Of course." When she stood unmoving— waiting for him to unveil his other forearm—he cocked his head in question. "I mean, sure. I'm going now. To start the car."

She almost fanned her face when she got in the driver's seat but caught herself just in time. What was she? Twelve? She was practically swooning over the man. *Have some dignity, Megan.* Besides, now was not the time. She had to get to the club. She couldn't be late for her performance. As she reached for the ignition switch, her eyes were drawn to something on the dashboard.

"No." She shook her head in denial. "Please, no."

But the fuel gauge revealed the truth about her predicament. Her car hadn't broken down. She apparently had forgotten to put gas in it. Megan lightly banged her head against the steering wheel. She'd chosen the worst day to fail at adulting.

"Is everything all right?"

Megan sat up with a surprised yelp. Right. The Good Samaritan. She'd been so busy beating herself up that she didn't even notice that he'd come to stand by her door.

"Yeah, um, hi." A fierce blush sprang to her cheeks.

"Hi." A corner of his lips quirked for a split second. "Are you okay?"

"I'm fine." She blew out a long breath. "But I'm an idiot. I know what's wrong with my car. It's out of gas."

His eyebrows shot up on his forehead, but his voice was judgment free when he said, "Well, I'm glad you figured out the problem."

"Yes. Thank you for stopping to help," she mumbled. Too embarrassed to meet his eyes, she grabbed her phone and opened her rideshare app. But she was in Los Angeles past nine o'clock on a Saturday. No driver would arrive in time to take her to Hollywood. "I'm so screwed."

"What's wrong?" That ghost of a smile touched his lips again as he added, "Other than being stranded on the side of the road."

"I'm supposed to perform at a club in Hollywood, but I don't think I'll be able to make it on time." She clicked on another app and sighed. "It's peak time for rideshares."

"I would offer to give you a lift, but I'm supposed to meet someone at the Chamber Music Society performance."

It was her turn to offer him a sympathetic smile. "Sorry, but that concert ended almost half an hour ago."

"Shit." He raked his fingers through his hair, straightening to his full height. After a moment, he said, "I guess that means I can give you a lift to Hollywood."

Accepting a ride from a complete stranger might be the dumbest thing she had done in her adult life, but the musician in her balked at the idea of missing her debut performance. And she trusted the man on a basic level—nothing in her was yelling "run for your life"—and her intuition was never wrong. Besides, tonight was about leaving her comfort zone and embarking on something new.

"I'm going to shamelessly take advantage of your

kindness." She caught her bottom lip between her teeth, hoping she wouldn't regret this.

"By all means," he said with a gracious nod.

Megan grabbed her violin and locked up her car. Luckily, it had stopped at a street that allowed parking from 9:00 p.m. to 6:00 a.m., so she could come back with a can of gas after the performance. They walked over to his Maserati and he opened the passenger door for her. She was oddly reassured by the old-fashioned gesture. Whoever heard of a criminal with good manners?

After tapping the Tipsy Dahlia into his navigation app, he maneuvered the car into the street. She took a moment to study his profile from under her lashes, her heart drumming in her chest. She couldn't remember the last time she'd been so attracted to a man—probably because she'd never been this attracted to anyone before. The magnetic pull he had on her was both heady and unnerving.

"You're not an ax murderer or anything, are you?" she asked to curb the lust simmering in her blood.

"Shouldn't you have asked me that before you got in my car?" He arched an eyebrow at her, amusement dancing in his eyes. A delicious shiver traveled down her back. "But no, I've never owned an ax."

She laughed and relaxed into her seat. "I'm Megan, by the way."

"I'm Daniel," he said, glancing sideways at her. His eyes lingered on her face and she felt heat rising to her cheeks. "Nice to meet you."

"Thank you for coming to my rescue." She looked down at her hands, suddenly feeling shy.

"My pleasure." His deep voice felt like a caress against her skin, and goose bumps spread on her arms. "May I ask what you're performing tonight?"

"Something I've never done before," she confessed. "I'm playing rock violin at the club."

"I'm intrigued," he said in a way that made her wonder if he was talking about her performance or *her*. "Is that your violin?"

"Yes, my electric violin." She patted the case she had tucked to one side of her legs. It was a glorious, edgy beauty—bright, shiny and red.

"I'm looking forward to hearing you play," he said.

"You're going to stay?" She couldn't hold back her grin.

"I can't think of a better way to spend the evening." He smiled back at her. It was a hint of a smile, really—small and slightly crooked—but it made her breath catch in her throat.

She shouldn't read anything into it. He was just curious about what a rock violin performance looked like. Well, she was curious, too, since she had never been to one herself, much less performed in one. Hopefully, she would make it there on time. She was certain she would lose her slot if she was late. The easy conversation in the car trickled to a stop as she anxiously stared at the dashboard clock.

"What time is your performance?" he asked.

"Ten." She squirmed a bit in her seat.

"We'll make it." His reassurance—and the slight

lurch of the car as he sped up—eased some of her worry.

They drove up to the front of the club at precisely three minutes before ten. Grabbing her violin, she opened the door and stepped one foot on the sidewalk.

She paused long enough to say, "Thank you so much."

Megan skidded inside the Tipsy Dahlia with two minutes to spare. She wasted a precious minute for her eyes to adjust to the bleary darkness. The club was small but it was jam-packed. She squeezed through the crowd of people, heading for what she hoped was the backstage area.

She made it there out of breath and pulled her violin from the case just as the MC announced, "And here to rock out on her violin with you…Megan."

She felt the familiar course of preperformance jitters and excitement flow through her as she walked out on the stage. Alone. The spotlight was so bright that she could hardly see anything. She looked over her shoulder, but her sisters weren't there to give her a reassuring smile or a warm squeeze of her hand.

Swallowing nervously, she turned her gaze back to the audience. The light was still blinding, but she let the roar of the crowd and the heat of their bodies wash over her. She took a slow, steadying breath. They wanted to hear her music and there was nothing she loved more than sharing it with the audience. She tucked her violin under her chin, her face splitting into a giant grin. She could do this.

Her performance was loud, messy and so damn

fun. The energy of the crowd zinged through her like electricity and she wove through the stage with her violin, her ponytail swishing back and forth with every bend and twist of her body. The music swelled around her and reached dizzying heights as she played the highest notes on the violin with frantic speed. Her audience's shouts became frenzied as she held them at the pinnacle for impossibly long seconds—channeling her favorite heavy-metal guitar solos—then she brought them crashing down only to gently lift them up again. When she finished, she threw her arms up to the ceiling, her bow and violin in each hand, and the crowd howled its approval.

"Thank you. You guys are awesome." High on adrenaline, she strode off the stage with her chest heaving and sweat dripping down her forehead.

She did it. She fucking nailed her first solo performance. She pressed an unsteady hand over her mouth as a sound between a sob and a laugh escaped from her. If felt incredible to stand on her own—just knowing that she could centered something inside her. She closed her eyes and took a deep breath to savor the moment.

"You were spectacular."

Megan swung around to find her gorgeous stranger leaning against the back wall with his arms crossed over his chest.

"You stayed," she whispered, surprised by how happy that made her.

"I told you I would." He pushed himself off the wall and walked toward her.

She hurriedly stowed away her violin and straightened to face him. "Why?"

He stopped a few feet away from her, his eyes raking her body with enough heat to burn her panties off. "For you."

Instinct was a funny thing. She had never attacked a man before, but she pounced on the stranger as though she'd done it a hundred times. She pressed her body against him like she wanted to meld with him, and her hands fisted in his thick hair as she crushed her mouth to his.

To his credit, he didn't hesitate before wrapping her leg around his waist, his other hand cupping her ass. Her lips parted on a moan, and his tongue invaded her mouth with swift authority. Her teeth clacked against his as she sucked him in deeper and tangled her tongue roughly with his.

She reminded herself that she'd spoken fewer than ten sentences with the man. She didn't even know his last name. But her body had taken over. She didn't give a damn that she was kissing a stranger as though her life depended on it as long as she got to keep doing it.

He hoisted her up by the waist and she wrapped her other leg around him, and he spun them around and pressed her back against the wall. Her breath left her on a sharp gasp when he cupped her breast with his large hand and kneaded it. She didn't hear the laughter or the clack of footsteps until he set her back on the ground, holding her firmly by her hips.

"Let's get out of here," he said in a gravelly voice, his chest rising and falling with each swift breath.

Megan didn't think she could form words, so she nodded. Something hot and hungry flared in his eyes, then he took her hand and sprinted toward the exit. She ran beside him with a smile lighting up her face. This surreal night would be something all her own.

One

Three months later

"Please don't tell me that's your lunch," Angie said with a disapproving glance at the bag of Sour Patch Kids.

Megan popped another piece into her mouth and chewed, swallowing down a wave of nausea. "Of course not. It's three o'clock. Who eats lunch at three?"

Now that she was nearing the second trimester of her pregnancy, her morning sickness—which was actually all-freaking-day sickness—was finally beginning to let up. She was able to tolerate a few spoons of soup for lunch, then she washed it down with half a can of Coke because water still tasted disgusting.

It was better than living solely off Sour Patch Kids and candied ginger like she had for the last couple of months.

"I worry about you. You've lost weight," her older sister fretted.

Megan smiled. She loved being fussed over by her unni. A part of her couldn't wait to tell her sisters about being pregnant so they could fuss their big ol' hearts out. But another part of her didn't want to worry them, because she planned on raising the baby on her own.

An image of the beautiful stranger flashed through her mind, but she pushed it aside. That was all he was. A stranger. Besides, it wasn't like she had any way of contacting him to let him know that she was pregnant. This baby was hers and hers alone.

She breathed to stop the now-familiar panic from taking hold. Having something all her own didn't feel like a sparkling treasure anymore. But she could do this—she had to for her baby. *My baby.* She remembered her performance at the Tipsy Dahlia—how amazing it felt to stand on her own. The thought reinforced her spine with steely confidence. *I can do this.*

"Especially since you didn't have any spare weight to lose in the first place," Chloe added. "It wouldn't be as big a deal if I dropped a few pounds."

Angie tsked. "You're lovely just as you are."

"I know." Her younger sister smiled, with her eyes twinkling. She really was very lovely. "I'm just saying Megan needs to start eating better."

"All right. Stop ganging up on me." Megan rolled

her eyes. Even before she got pregnant, her sisters had been on her case about her candy addiction. "I'll eat real food. Satisfied?"

"Yes." Angie nodded. "Ready to get to work?"

"Let's do this," Chloe said, lifting her viola to her chin. "We haven't played this piece in months. It's going to need some work."

Megan and her sisters practiced three times a week in a room they rented at the local community college. With the new season fast approaching, they would need to rehearse even more often. *The new season.* She was going to start showing soon. She couldn't help but wonder if her pregnancy would affect her career in any way. Many of the Chamber Music Society's patrons were quite conservative. Would they frown upon her single-mom status?

And she would have to miss some performances because the baby was due before the end of the season. The Hana Trio wouldn't be a trio without her… She would worry about that when the time came but she couldn't put off telling her sisters much longer.

The rehearsal was a welcome distraction from her cluttered thoughts. Playing with her sisters—even when they were practicing the same few bars over and over again—always made her happy. The music seemed to chase away the lingering morning sickness. By the end of practice, she felt better than she had in months.

"Yup," Megan said while putting away her violin, "this piece definitely needs more work."

"But I think we made good progress today," Angie pointed out.

"Agreed." Chloe stood from her chair and shouldered her viola case. "We'll have it perfected by opening night."

After hugging each of her sisters much longer than necessary, Megan walked out to her car and ventured onto the congested freeway for her drive home. Describing rush hour in Los Angeles as heavy traffic was a gross understatement. *Traffic* implied that there was some movement. No, the freeways felt more like a giant parking lot. Her playlist was the only thing that kept Megan sane through her commute.

While she was a classically trained musician, her playlist consisted mostly of rock and heavy metal. She sincerely believed that her love of that genre made her a better musician, especially with so much classical influence in heavy metal. And it definitely helped her interpret her rock violin pieces more authentically. Not that she had performed at any more clubs since that first night. A wistful sigh escaped her.

It hadn't been possible for her to perform her electric violin with her unrelenting morning sickness. But even before that, she didn't go out of her way to book another gig. She might or might not have been avoiding another chance encounter with *him*. She didn't know what the etiquette of a one-night stand was, but sneaking out of the hotel room in the cover of darkness seemed like a dick move—a dick move she had pulled.

How could she have known that his last name or a phone number would've come in handy a few weeks later when she peed on a stick or two? Fine, five. She peed on five sticks. Regardless, she'd made a decision—mostly out of panic and mortification, but it was still her decision to run away—and now she had to live with the rather significant consequence of raising a child on her own.

But her decision to become a mother at this point in her life was not a *consequence* but a *choice*. She lived in a state where abortions were legal so she had the freedom to make that important, personal choice for herself. It infuriated her that she felt grateful for it—that there was a very real threat that such a basic human right could be taken away from her…from every person who could become pregnant. She blew out a long, frustrated breath.

Megan survived her drive home and parked in the garage with a deep sigh. The moment she opened the door leading into the house, the aroma of a Korean feast assailed her nostrils—soy sauce, garlic, sesame oil—and she didn't hate it. In fact, her stomach growled raucously and her mouth watered because everything smelled…delicious. Did this mean her morning sickness was over?

In her excitement over the prospect of eating a proper meal, it slipped her mind that her dad had mentioned having a business associate over for dinner. So when she barged into the living room, she was doubly shocked to discover a stranger sitting on the sectional with her dad—not just any stranger but *her* stranger.

What in the ever-loving hell?

The stranger shot to his feet, his expression a mixture of shock, anger and a hint of something she couldn't identify. Then everything was wiped clean and replaced by polite indifference, making her doubt whether any of the emotions were ever there.

"Ah, Megan. You're home," her dad said, turning to face her. She scrambled to close her gaping mouth but couldn't hide her bewilderment in time. Grooves of concern formed over the bridge of his nose. "Did you forget we were having a dinner guest?"

"Yes...we're so busy preparing for the new season," she managed. *How is this happening?* "Please forgive me."

"I'm Daniel Pak." Their guest walked up to her and extended his hand. "Nice to meet you."

So they were going to pretend to be complete strangers... That was probably a good call on his part. He couldn't exactly say, "Hey, didn't we sleep together a few months ago?" in front of her dad. God, she was unravelling.

"Megan Han." She plastered on a fake smile by sheer force of will and gave him a firm handshake. The jolt of electricity that shot down her spine was hard to ignore and only added to her panic. "It's a pleasure to meet you."

Daniel held on to her hand for a second too long and she wondered what that meant. Was he happy to see her again? Or was it a warning not to tell her dad anything? *Right.* If she could guess what the man was thinking by an extra second of hand shaking then she was in the wrong profession. She felt hysterical laughter bubble in her throat.

"Daniel is—" her dad began.

"I'm going to see if Mrs. Chung needs any help with dinner," Megan practically shouted over him and rushed out of the living room.

In a daze, she climbed the stairs to her room. Who the hell was he? How did he know her dad? *Oh God. Do I have to tell him about the baby?* She closed her bedroom door and leaned back against it. She didn't know what to do.

Her fist clenched around the handle of her violin case, reminding her she needed to put it away. After taking a deep breath, she pushed off the door and set her violin down beside her music stand. Hiding in her room wouldn't solve anything. If she wanted answers, she had to go back downstairs and join her dad and their guest for dinner. Then she could decide how she felt about this chance encounter—their second one.

She walked into her closet and clicked on the light. Both her dad and Daniel were wearing dress shirts and slacks, so she was a bit underdressed in her leggings and oversize T-shirt. She changed into a pale blue blouse and pulled a black pencil skirt off the hanger. But when she stepped into it and lifted it over her hips, she could barely close the zipper halfway up.

"Shit," she muttered.

Even though she'd lost weight over the last couple months, a soft bump pushed insistently from her lower stomach. Soon, none of her clothes would fit her. But her frustration quickly morphed into a tenderness that still surprised her. She placed her hand over her stomach and smiled down at her changing body. How could she love someone she hadn't even met yet?

Her smile faltered and a frisson of nerves ran through her. The baby's father was waiting downstairs for her…and she had to tell him about the baby. How would he react to the news? She shook her head before any disastrous scenarios could take root in her mind. It didn't matter. He had a right to know. With calm resolve, she changed into a cream shift dress and headed for the kitchen.

"Hi, Mrs. Chung," Megan said, her eyes going round at the sight of all the delectable food. Mrs. Chung had been her family's housekeeper for as long as she could remember. With both her sisters out of the house—Chloe had decided to live on campus while she finished her master's—and her dad working long hours, Megan would've been lonely if it hadn't been for Mrs. Chung. "Do you need any help?"

"No, I'm fine. Thank you for asking, my dear," she said, placing bite-size pieces of egg-battered cod on the frying pan. "I just need to finish frying up this last batch of jeon."

Megan snagged one of the fish jeon resting in a wicker platter and popped it in her mouth. Her eyes slid shut at the savory, umami goodness. "Mmm."

"Do you have your appetite back?" Mrs. Chung's eyebrows rose in surprise. "You've hardly eaten the last couple months."

"Yeah, um, it's just been too hot this summer," Megan said, avoiding her eyes. She would have to tell everyone eventually—starting with Daniel tonight—

but first, she was going to fortify herself with some food. She popped another piece of fish in her mouth while she schooled her features. "I guess I have more of an appetite now that it's finally cooling down. I should, um, set the table."

When everything was ready, her dad took a seat at the head of the table. Megan studiously avoided staring at Daniel as they sat down across from each other on either side of her dad. The dinner was more relaxed and casual than the slightly stuffy business affairs her dad occasionally held at their home. The two men shared a rapport that would've piqued her curiosity if she wasn't so preoccupied with her own predicament.

Unable to stop herself, she glanced at Daniel from under her lashes. Her dad didn't invite just anyone over for dinner at their house. They had to be of some significance to Jigu Corporation. Who was he? What was his relationship to her dad? Her eyes narrowed as a sudden thought occurred to her. Had he known she was Minsung Han's daughter when he approached her that night? What game was he playing at?

In all fairness, Daniel wasn't playing any games with her at the dinner table. He certainly didn't send any secret, significant glances her way. He paid her just enough attention not to be impolite but he didn't seem the least bit interested in her. She covered her huff of annoyance by stuffing some bulgogi in her mouth. What did she care about capturing his interest? She had bigger things to worry about. But her eyes kept straying toward him—the darn man was as gorgeous as he'd been the night she'd first met him.

"Daniel joined Jigu Corporation as the new Chief Financial Officer a few months back," her dad addressed her.

She froze with her hand over the japchae, and the slippery vermicelli noodles slid straight off her chopsticks. *You've got to be kidding me.* Her one-night stand worked for her dad? It would've been bad enough if he was some business associate in town for a few days. But him being a long-term fixture at her dad's company made things so much worse. Her pregnancy could wreak havoc on the situation if she didn't tread carefully.

How had someone so young become the CFO anyway? He couldn't be more than a couple years older than her. Then again, she was a twenty-seven-year-old who constantly got carded when ordering drinks. Maybe he just looked younger than he was. Even so, he couldn't be older than thirty.

"Oh?" She hid her surprise and resumed transferring the noodles to her plate. "The same CFO who didn't show up at our last concert?"

"My apologies," Daniel interjected smoothly. "I got detained with an urgent matter at work. By the time I got to the concert hall, the performance had already ended."

"That's a shame," she murmured.

"Yes," he said with a slight arch of his eyebrow, "but I was fortunate enough to catch another performance that evening, which I quite enjoyed."

"Is that so?" She fell miles short of cool indifference as her cheeks flushed with pleasure. She cleared her throat and looked down at her plate. "I didn't even realize the CFO position was open."

"I begged Jerry to hold off his retirement until we found someone perfect for the job." Her dad raised his glass to the young CFO with a playful wink. "He sure was glad when Daniel came along."

Megan's eyes widened despite herself. *Perfect?* Her dad held himself and others to ridiculously high standards. She'd never heard him describe anyone or anything as *perfect* before.

"I'm hardly perfect, Mr. Han," Daniel said with a hint of a smile.

"Don't sell yourself short. You've more than proven your competence during your time at the East Coast office. You single-handedly revamped the business development department in one year. That's no small feat. Jigu needs that kind of passion and vision at the executive level," her dad said, clapping Daniel on the shoulder. "Besides, the board of directors wouldn't have approved your appointment if they didn't believe you were qualified."

She couldn't believe the bromance vibes she was getting. She stared at her dad, but he busied himself piling more food onto his plate, urging their guest to do the same.

"Thank you. I appreciate your faith in me." Daniel regarded her dad with undisguised respect. "But we have to remember that not everyone was thrilled about my appointment as the new CFO."

"Don't worry about that." Her dad waved aside the younger man's concern. "You'll win them over soon enough."

What in the world was going on? It was hard enough figuring out what it meant to have Daniel back in her life. But now she had to contend with the fact that he and her dad had a close connection that she knew nothing about. Megan had a sinking feeling that things were about to get much more complicated.

Daniel tasted nothing as he methodically shoveled food into his mouth, chewed and swallowed. He nodded and chuckled along with Mr. Han's anecdotes without really hearing him. He was too busy *feeling* Megan sitting across from him, with every molecule in his body. Once everything sank in, he knew he'd be more concerned with the fact that she was Min-sung Han's daughter—that he'd slept with the CEO's daughter—but for now, he couldn't stop his heart from racing with the thrill of being in the same room as her.

A headache was building up in his temples from all the effort it took to keep his eyes off her. But if he looked at her, he might not be able to hold back the longing and frustration he'd been suppressing for the last three months. She'd probably hoped to never see him again when she snuck out of the hotel room that night. He had convinced himself that he had no problem with that. At least he thought he had. But with her only a few feet away from him, he wasn't so sure anymore.

Daniel finally allowed himself to steal a glimpse of

her as they moved from the dining room back to the living room. She was even more beautiful than he'd remembered. Her silky black hair fell past her shoulders and her face was clear of makeup other than the rosy sheen of her lips. She looked thinner, though. His eyebrows drew together.

After a dessert of sliced apples, pears and tea, Mr. Han made a show of yawning loudly. "This old man needs to turn in for the night…"

Daniel got to his feet. "I should head out."

"Why are you in such a hurry to get back to your empty condo?" The older man placed a hand on his shoulder. "You two should chat a while longer. As they say, the night is still young."

Daniel lowered himself back onto the sofa and glanced at Megan. She gaped at Mr. Han as though she was wondering who the hell he was and what he'd done with her father.

"Appa…" she began.

"Keep him company and get to know him a little," Mr. Han cajoled with a wide smile. "He's part of the Jigu family now."

All Mr. Han needed to do was give them an exaggerated wink to make it any more obvious that he was playing matchmaker. Daniel was touched that he would trust one of his daughters to him. And he felt horrible that he had betrayed his trust even before it was given to him. Minsung Han was his mentor and his friend. What would he think if he knew that Daniel had had a one-night stand with Megan?

"Good night." With a wave over his shoulder, Mr.

Han walked out of the living room, leaving the two of them alone.

"Do you have any idea what that was all about?" Megan turned to Daniel in a huff.

"No clue." He leaned back on the couch and crossed his arms over his chest. "Now, I have a question for you."

She opened her mouth, then closed it. After staring intently at her lap for a few seconds, she met his gaze. "Not here. There's a café nearby. I'll meet you at the door in two minutes."

He watched her leave the room, unable to stop himself from taking in the sway of her hips and the soft curve of her calves. He couldn't deny that he still wanted her, but she was off-limits now. Getting involved with the CEO's daughter was asking for trouble, especially when he was only good for a casual fling. Experience told him that women didn't stick around, so it was better to not give them any permanence in his life. He swiped a hand down his face and headed for the front door. She joined him shortly with a purse hooked on her arm.

"Do you want to drive together?" she asked, stepping out the door he held open for her. "It's not far. I'll grab a rideshare back home after we chat."

"Sure," he said. She quirked an eyebrow at him as though she knew he had every intention of bringing her home himself.

They arrived at the small café after a short, silent drive—she'd seemed lost in thought and he'd kept his eyes on the road. After ordering their drinks at the counter, they sat at a corner table which allowed them some privacy.

"Okay." Megan wrapped her hands around her mug as though she needed comfort. "Ask me."

"Why did you leave without a word that night?" He allowed his expression to betray no more than mild curiosity even though he was holding his breath, waiting for her answer.

"I, um—" she ran her fingertip around the rim of her mug "—kind of freaked out."

"Freaked out?" he repeated slowly, his eyebrow arching in bewilderment.

"I've never done something like that," she said. When his eyes widened, she clicked her tongue. "Not sex. I've had sex before…although I had no idea that sex could be like *that*. But that's not the point."

How could he notice how adorable she was at a time like this? He overcompensated for the smile he was fighting by drawing his lips down into a grim line.

"The point is I've never had sex with a complete stranger before," she continued. "I didn't even know your last name…"

"Do you usually deal with novel situations by running away?" He didn't like the hint of bitterness in his tone. What was wrong with him? They'd slept together once. He had no claim on her. But as much as he hated to admit it, it stung that she'd been ready to never see him again.

"Judge all you want, but I do *not* make a habit of running away from my problems," she said, tilting her chin up. "My turn. Did you know who I was when we met that night?"

"What? Know you how?" Then he realized what she was asking and his eyes narrowed with a flash of anger. "Are you implying that I deliberately approached you because you're Minsung Han's daughter?"

"To be honest, I see no reason for you to have done that," she stated matter-of-factly. "I have to believe that this is just a bizarre, unfortunate coincidence."

He pinched the bridge of his nose. He agreed that it was bizarre, but he wasn't sure if it was unfortunate. Even if one night was all he got with her, he didn't regret it.

"Damn it. I offended you." She sighed, her shoulders drooping. "It really doesn't help me to offend you right now. I just needed to make sure you didn't have any nefarious, alternative motives for sleeping with me that night—other than lust. Because I'm fine with lust."

"I'm glad you approve of lust." A corner of his lips twitched against his volition. "But why do you need to rule out…what was it?…*nefarious, alternative motives*?"

"Because I have something to tell you and I can't have you using the information against me or my father."

He paused with his mug halfway to his lips. "What do you have to tell me?"

"I'm pregnant," she said.

His mug slammed back on the table, sloshing hot

coffee on his hand, but Daniel didn't feel a thing as her words sank in and his world tilted.

I'm going to be a father.

Two

Megan braced herself for the usual line of questions men asked in these situations. She had no personal experience, but she'd seen enough TV shows and movies to know what to expect. She could handle the angry denials and accusations. She had a third-degree black belt in verbal sparring.

Daniel wiped the spilled coffee off the table with care, then stared intently down at his hands. His quiet contemplation stretched on until she wanted to squirm in her seat. She felt like she'd showed up for battle—loins girded—only to find her enemy pouring tea for them on a linen-covered table. When he looked up at last, her stomach lurched with nerves. What was he thinking?

"Marry me," he said in a low, even voice.

She almost fell out of her chair.

"What?" she shouted before clapping her hand over her mouth. He couldn't have said what she thought he'd said. She glanced around the café to make sure no one noticed and said in a much softer voice, "What?"

"I want you to marry me." He nodded as though his bonkers proposal sounded even better to him the second time around.

"Aren't you... Aren't you going to ask me if I'm sure the baby is yours?" she said weakly.

"Based on your *freak-out*, you're not someone who engages in casual sex," he observed. "And you don't seem like a person who would cheat on someone you're in a relationship with."

"But we used a condom," she argued on his behalf.

"Two condoms. I recall having you twice," he murmured.

Her heart fluttered in response to his barely there smile, and the memory of their night together made heat gather low in her stomach.

"Why are you so calm?" She glared at him, suddenly finding his composure infuriating when she was all aflutter and horny to boot.

"I'm asking a woman I'm meeting for the second time to marry me. I'm far from calm," he said, sounding as calm as could be. "But this is how *I* respond to novel situations. By analyzing the facts and choosing the most logical course of action, which, in this case, is taking responsibility for my actions."

"*Our* actions," she corrected. "But that's not the

point. You don't have to take responsibility for anything. This is my body, my baby, my responsibility."

"That makes no sense." His eyebrows furrowed
over the bridge of his nose. "If it's *our* actions then
it's *our* baby, *our* responsibility—"

"I'm only telling you because you have the right
to know." She cut him off and held up a finger when
he opened his mouth. "If you want…you can be a
part of the child's life. But a loveless marriage is out
of the question."

Icy disdain hardened his features. "Marriage doesn't
have to be about love."

"Well, marriage shouldn't be about responsibility
and duty," she countered, her voice rising in indigna-
tion. A happy marriage was all about love. She'd seen
it with her parents and now with Angie and Joshua.

"Responsibility and duty are far more reliable than
love," he bit out.

The finality of his statement chilled her. What happened to him to make him balk at the idea of love?
Had someone hurt him in the past? It was none of
her business. Everyone had their emotional baggage.
Besides, it wasn't like she was going to marry him. It
didn't matter what he thought about love.

"We'll have to agree to disagree on that one," she
said quietly.

He held her gaze for a moment, then nodded once.
The hard edge left his expression when he asked,
"Does your father know you're pregnant?"

"No." She shook her head. "I haven't told anyone
yet."

"He championed me to become Jigu Corporation's CFO, and I repay him by getting his daughter pregnant," Daniel scoffed and swiped a weary hand down his face. "How could I have betrayed his trust like this?"

"It's not like we had unprotected sex." She wanted to ease his remorse. Neither of them had intended to step into this complicated mess. "Besides, you didn't even know who I was."

"That doesn't change the fact that you're pregnant with my child," he said with a hint of possessiveness that made her stomach dip.

"What do you want me to do?" Her voice was barely above a whisper.

"I already told you." He swooped in like a hawk diving for its prey. "I want you to marry me."

She blinked rapidly. Marrying him would make life so much easier. She wouldn't have to worry about disappointing her dad, being a single mom or the potential censure of the classical music community. But... she couldn't compromise on love. She wouldn't. And she could stand on her own—not only to perform rock violin but in life. She knew that now.

"Please stop saying that. We're not getting married." She smiled to soften her words even though he was only proposing out of a misplaced sense of duty. "Other than that...what do you want from me?"

"Nothing I can have again." There was no denying the heat in his eyes.

Her breath caught in her throat and warmth gathered between her legs. He still wanted her, and if her body's reaction was any indication, she very much wanted him back. But he was right. They couldn't give in to their attraction. Things were complicated enough without them picking up where they'd left off.

"This is a lot for us to process all at once," she said, suddenly exhausted. "Let's take some time to think things through before we decide how we want to handle this. I'll hold off on telling my father anything for the time being."

"Are you finally going to give me your number?" he asked wryly.

She rolled her eyes and held out her hand. When he reached into his pocket and handed her his phone, she tapped in her number and pressed Dial. An East Coast number popped up on her screen.

"There." She returned his phone. "Now we both have each other's number."

"Good," he said, rising to his feet. "Let me take you home."

"There's no need. I'll get a rideshare."

With an impatient click of his tongue, Daniel unhooked her purse from the back of her chair and walked off.

"Hey," she protested, even though she had no choice but to follow.

He waited by his car, holding the passenger-side door open. She caught up with him with unhurried steps. His high-handed stunt annoyed her, but she had a feeling there were many more battles ahead of them. He could have this tiny victory as long as she won the big ones.

* * *

After exchanging a ridiculously courteous goodnight with Daniel—she had no idea how to behave with her one-night stand turned secret baby daddy—Megan went straight to her dad's study and knocked. She knew he hadn't *turned in early*. He was a night owl like her.

"Come in," he said.

She pushed open the door and found him typing away on his laptop with his reading glasses perched on his nose. Even by the soft lamplight, she could see how much his hair had grayed in the last few years. He had always worked long hours, but that was all he seemed to do since her mom died.

"Do you have a minute?" she asked, settling down on an armchair.

He responded with a rush of typing, then came to join her in the sitting area. "What is it?"

"I wanted to talk to you about Daniel." She wanted to find out more about the connection the two men shared that she'd detected earlier in the evening. And if she were being honest with herself, she was more than mildly curious about the father of her baby. "Are you guys...close?"

"Why do you ask?" Her dad took off his glasses and wiped the lenses with the end of his shirt, trying to hide the smile playing around his mouth. "Did you have a nice time with him?"

"Appa, I'm being serious."

"And I'm not?" His grin grew wider. "He's a good man. Smart, loyal and decent."

"Hmm." There it was again—the high praise. She pursed her lips. "I just got the feeling that he was more than a valued employee."

"Well, that depends. Are you seeing him again?"

"Stop it." She stood from her seat. Her dad was in an odd mood, and she wasn't getting anywhere with him. "You're a horrible matchmaker."

"I want you to give it some thought." His expression turned serious as he got to his feet. "I'm grooming him to take over Jigu Corporation when I retire. It would be nice to keep the business in the family."

Too shocked to reply, Megan nodded and left his study. She replayed her conversation with her dad as she went through her nighttime routine. He was preparing Daniel to become Jigu's next CEO. He'd dedicated all of his adult life to the company and loved it like an extension of himself. He really must trust Daniel.

She lay down in bed and stared up at the ceiling. Fate must have a twisted sense of humor. Her dad valued loyalty above all else. He would be livid if he found out Daniel had had a one-night stand with her and got her pregnant. He would see it as a betrayal and an affront to their family's honor. But then he would quickly see the situation as his matchmaking dream come true and try to force them to get married. Well, force *her* to marry Daniel since the man was already prepared to embrace matrimony out of duty.

She couldn't allow that to happen.

It was true this baby was unexpected, but that didn't mean she had to give up on love and happily ever after. She placed a gentle hand on her stomach.

No, it meant that she had to fight harder for her dreams now because her baby's happiness depended on it, too.

Daniel yawned into his sixth cup of coffee. His week had passed in a blur of meetings. He was relieved when his dinner meeting was canceled—he desperately needed a break from schmoozing—so he could continue familiarizing himself with his actual duties as the CFO. But it was past eight o'clock in the evening and the words on the screen were beginning to blur.

He rubbed his eyes with his thumb and index finger until the stinging subsided and leaned back in his chair. Even in the midst of his hectic week, Megan had never been far from his mind—Megan and the baby. His stomach clenched nervously. *Their* baby.

Marriage and children had not been a part of his plans—even before Sienna's betrayal. He swept aside the intrusive thought. His parents' marriage was a patented disaster, based on his memory of the wreck his father had been when his mother left them. His father hadn't been able to look at Daniel without remembering his mother—his gaze filled with a mixture of loss and resentment. He had wondered countless times whether his father regretted having him. He rubbed his chest as a cold hollowness spread inside him. If his father hadn't loved his mother—and been utterly devastated when their marriage ended—then maybe he would've been able to love Daniel more.

No, marriage and children had never factored into his goals. He wanted to become a formidable figure in his field and earn the respect of his peers. He wanted to prove to the world that he was someone valuable—someone they couldn't toss aside. But planned or not, he refused to bring a child into this world and have them feel unwanted.

Daniel pushed himself away from his desk and paced the length of his office. He wanted to raise his child in a home with both a mother and a father—maybe because he'd never had that. A marriage based on responsibility and duty meant that no one would get their heart broken. Their love for their child would never be tainted by bitterness and resentment. Why couldn't Megan see that?

He dragged his fingers through his hair. He couldn't force her to marry him, but there were other ways for him to be in his child's life. He would make sure they knew that they were wanted and loved. Always.

Daniel retrieved his phone from his desk and texted Megan.

We need to talk.

Fortunately for his sanity, ellipses started rolling immediately after he hit Send.

I agree. When and where?

His thumbs flew over his phone.

In forty-five minutes. At the café we met last week.

He didn't wait for her response and grabbed his jacket from the coat hanger. Even if rush hour was over, it was going to take him at least thirty minutes to get to the café. He had a fifteen-minute cushion, but he didn't want to keep Megan waiting. His phone dinged as he stepped out of his office and headed toward the elevators.

See you soon.

The traffic was heavier than he would've liked and he pulled into the café's parking lot with only five minutes to spare. After he got out of his car, he saw Megan near the entrance and sprinted to catch up with her.

"Megan," he said, grabbing the door handle before her.

"Oh." She placed her hand over her chest. "You startled me. Where did you come from?"

"Sorry." He wanted to smack his forehead. "I was right behind you."

"That's fine. No big deal," she said, walking in through the door.

He followed her inside and headed for the counter. "What would you like?"

"Decaf Moroccan mint tea, please." She came to stand beside him.

"Why don't you go have a seat? I'll bring the drinks over when they're ready."

She shrugged and headed for the corner table they occupied last time. When he joined her with two mugs, she smiled at him. "Thank you."

"My pleasure." He caught himself staring at her

and quickly took a sip of his green tea, scalding his tongue and the roof of his mouth.

"I'm glad you reached out to me," she said. "I wanted to talk to you, but I didn't want to bother you. My father said you had a hectic week at work."

He bit back a curse. She'd been waiting to hear back from him. "I'm sorry for taking so long."

"No worries." She blew on her tea before she took a careful sip.

Megan seemed more relaxed than the last time he saw her, and being near her calmed him somehow. The thought of becoming a father still made his stomach flip over, but maybe they could make this work.

"I'm going to take a wild guess," he said. "You still don't want to marry me."

"Bingo." She winked.

His heart stuttered like a needle skipping on a vinyl record. He curled his hands into fists on his thighs to stop himself from grabbing her from across the table and kissing her senseless. She looked expectantly at him as though he was capable of speech. When he continued staring wordlessly at her, she cocked her head to the side.

"I guess I'll go first," she said after a moment. "We can't tell my father that the baby is yours."

"What? That's unacceptable." That did the job of snapping him out of his wink-induced stupor. "I can't lie to your father."

"We won't lie to him." She drew little circles on the table. "We'll just omit the truth."

"Which is the same as lying."

"What are you? A Boy Scout?" She narrowed her eyes at him. "Look, my father can be...hardheaded. If he finds out that I'm pregnant with your baby—as a result of a one-night stand—he will kill you. Then he'll resurrect you and kill you again for good measure."

He couldn't hold back his cringe. "I think you're exaggerating."

Megan arched an eyebrow and silently held his gaze.

"Slightly," he amended, remembering his mentor's hot temper.

"And he'll try to force us to get married." She held up her hand when he opened his mouth. "Uh-uh. No marriage. At any rate, if we refuse to join hands in holy matrimony, he might even fire you."

"Then, so be it," he said, even as his heart sank.

"Look, I know you worked hard to be here." She leaned closer to him and a waft of her sweet scent teased him. "It's not something you should throw away lightly."

His hand tightened around his mug. "I'm not doing any of this lightly, Megan."

Being Jigu Corporation's future CEO was his dream. He'd vowed to dedicate himself to carrying on Jigu's legacy. It would gut him to lose this opportunity, but he couldn't betray Mr. Han.

"I'm not saying we should keep him in the dark forever. I just need time to figure out a way to break the news to him without making him lose his senses." She lowered her voice. "I have a feeling my father won't do anything rash once the baby arrives and captures his heart."

His lips quirked despite himself. "You're going to use our baby to shield us from your father's wrath?"

"*Use* sounds a bit cold… Wait." Her eyelashes fluttered. "Our baby? So you've decided? You want to be a part of…our baby's life?"

"Yes." He swallowed against the tightness in his throat. "I want to be part of their life. Every moment of their life."

"I… I'm glad," she said with a tremulous smile.

"Me, too." His eyes flickered to her lips, but he forced his attention back to the issue at hand. "But about your father—"

"We'll tell him," she interrupted. "Just not yet. Think about it. What will happen if you get fired from Jigu? Can you guarantee that you'll be able to find a comparable job in LA? If you have to move away, you're going to miss so much of the baby's life."

"Hell."

She was right. Losing his position at Jigu Corporation meant he would have to find another job. Depending on the company, that might take him across the country. He didn't like it—he actually hated it—but maybe they should wait to tell her father.

"We'll revisit this issue soon," he said, raking his fingers through his hair.

"Okay." She nodded several times in quick succession. "I promise."

"So…" He blew out a long breath, leaning back in his seat. "How should we do this?"

"Do what?" She wrinkled her nose in confusion.

He waved his hand between them as he searched for the right words. "Be there for the baby. Together."

"Ah," she said with a small smile. "You mean co-parenting?"

"Yes, coparenting." He held back an answering smile. "We would probably need to see each other fairly often."

"I would assume so."

The thought of spending time with Megan appealed to him much more than was wise. He stomped down on the thrill of anticipation and muttered to remind himself, "All behind your father's back."

She shrugged helplessly. "For now, yes."

"Only until we figure out a way to tell him without getting my ass fired," he added. "We're not waiting for the baby to arrive."

"Okay." Megan pressed a hand to her stomach. "Honestly, it makes me sick to keep the truth from my father. I'm all for finding a solution as soon as possible."

His chest constricted at her distress. This wasn't an easy situation for either of them—especially for her. And if they weren't careful, things could get even more difficult.

"We need to acknowledge some things before we proceed," he said, holding her gaze. "I want you."

Her lips parted on a sharp indrawn breath and his groin tightened. Then she nodded with wide eyes, acknowledging his desire or admitting her own—he wasn't sure.

"But we can't act on this attraction." Sleeping with her, knowing who she was, would be a betrayal of Mr. Han's trust. Keeping the truth from him was betrayal enough. "We can't add more lies to our deception."

"No, we can't," she said in a small voice, her guilt plain on her face. "We…we could be partners. Coparenting partners. Nothing more."

"Agreed." He ignored the bewildering disappointment inside him. "We'll be partners."

They sat in silence for a while, staring down at their drinks. When he glanced up, his eyes caught on her bottom lip, which she worried between her teeth. He swallowed and resolutely shifted his focus to her forehead. As lovely as it was, it seemed safer than staring into her beautiful eyes, which were dangerously close to her plump pink lips.

"Tell me what you need," he blurted. He had no idea how to be there for Megan and the baby at this stage. "I mean…is there anything I can do for you? Do you have any doctor's appointments coming up?"

"It's still a couple of weeks away, but yeah, I do." She cleared her throat. "It's actually a pretty important appointment. The doctor's going to do an ultrasound and…she'll be able to tell us the sex of the baby."

The café spun ever so slightly around him. "The sex of the baby?"

"Yeah, it's pretty wild." She giggled a bit nervously. "It's going to make things feel so…real."

"Do you mind if I go with you?" Truthfully, the thought of seeing the baby for the first time—and finding out their sex—scared the shit out of him, but he wouldn't miss it for the world.

"No, not at all. I could use the moral support," she said shyly.

"I could do that. Give you moral support."

"Thank you." She hesitated before she continued, "If you don't want to find out the sex of the baby, we could wait…"

"Oh." He considered it for a moment. "I think I'd like to know. What about you?"

"Me, too."

They shared a smile. It felt good making decisions about their baby together. It felt really good.

"What else do you need?" he asked, feeling motivated. "Do you have any cravings?"

"Hmm." She scrunched her mouth to one side. "Not really. I'm just glad to be done with morning sickness. Until a week or so ago, I couldn't even drink water."

He wished he could've been there for her. "That sounds horrible."

"Yeah, it was." She wrinkled her nose.

"Well, if you get any cravings, let me know."

"Why? Do you plan on being my personal food delivery service?" she teased.

He chuckled. "If you'd like."

"Well, you asked for it. Don't come crying when I demand potato chips and ice cream at one in the morning."

"Maybe I should set up business hours," he said.

She tilted her head back and laughed. He was surprised at how much he enjoyed the sound. He tore his eyes away from her shining face and swallowed a mouthful of his lukewarm tea. He needed to get his attraction for her under control. They were coparenting partners now.

Even without their *agreement*, he had to remember that she'd walked out of the hotel room—and out of his life—without so much as a goodbye. If it wasn't for the baby, she wouldn't have wanted anything to do with him. He couldn't forget that.

Daniel had to tread carefully. Under different circumstances, he would have avoided spending time with her at all costs. Since that wasn't an option, he had to use every ounce of his self-control to remember that Megan Han was off-limits for him.

Three

After checking her phone for the twentieth time, Megan slapped it facedown on the table and took big gulps of her ice water. Her dad was even later than usual for their dinner date. If she hadn't been dying to try the new French bistro, she might've been tempted to leave. The cozy atmosphere with rich draperies and candlelit tables helped soothe her growing impatience, but if he wasn't there in ten minutes, she was going to order without him.

"Megan?" a familiar voice said from her side.

"Daniel?" She looked up at him in surprise. "What are you doing here?"

"I'm supposed to have dinner with your father, but I got held up at work." He scanned the restaurant.

"It doesn't look like he's here yet. Will you be joining us?"

Daniel glanced down at the table with confusion, drawing his eyebrows together. She was sitting at a table for two. Megan barely managed to hold back her groan. It went against every ounce of the filial piety engrained in her, but she was going to kill her dad when she got home.

"Why don't you sit down, Daniel?" She sighed and picked up the menu. A part of her didn't want to give in to her dad's matchmaking trickery, but she was hungry and she wasn't about to forego the chance to eat at the exclusive restaurant. "It's going to be just you and me for dinner tonight."

His frown cleared as he caught on to Minsung Han's clumsy attempt at playing Cupid. Daniel sat across from her with a bemused smile. "Not very subtle, is he?"

Megan snorted. "Not when it comes to matchmaking, I guess."

His eyes widened as though realizing something. "I kept you waiting for a while. I apologize. You must be starving."

"Apology accepted." She gave a one-shouldered shrug. "You didn't even know I'd be here."

"Even so."

"Everything sounds delicious." She changed the subject, noting that Daniel tended to be hard on himself. "I think I'm going to go for the tasting menu with white truffles."

"I'll have the same," he said, setting aside his menu.

"Good choice. It's nice and expensive." When he cocked his head in question, she explained, "It's going to be my father's treat. I'm whipping out his black card for pulling this stunt."

"Well, thank you for dinner, Mr. Han." Daniel raised his glass in mock salute.

Her phone buzzed and Megan snatched it off the table. It could only be one person. Her missing dinner date.

I'm sorry for the no show, but I sent you a younger, better looking dinner companion. Bon appetit!

"This is so embarrassing," she huffed her outrage and stuffed her phone into her purse with more force than necessary. "I'll have a talk with my father and make sure he doesn't try something like this again."

"Don't worry about it," he soothed. "Let's just pretend we ran into each other by coincidence."

"Sure, why not." She snapped her cloth napkin open and spread it across her lap. "We seem to do that a lot anyway."

"Do what a lot?"

"Run into each other by coincidence." Her face flushed the moment the words left her mouth. Would he think she was alluding to their first night together?

Before the moment could turn awkward, their server appeared at their table and they placed their orders.

"Would you like to do the wine pairing with the tasting menu?" the server asked.

Daniel shot a quick glance at her before answering, "No, thank you."

When their server left, she leaned toward Daniel and said softly, "You could do the wine pairing. I really don't mind."

"Neither do I. I'd much rather offer you my moral support." His full lips quirked at one corner.

"That's very considerate of you," she murmured.

Before she realized what she was doing, she reached across the table and placed her hand on top of his. Daniel turned his hand over and linked his fingers through hers without missing a beat. Then he looked down at their hands as though he had no idea how that had happened. But he didn't break the contact and neither did she, even as heat spread up her arm and through her body.

"Megan?"

Walter Liu, an old family friend and a member of Jigu Corporation's board of directors, walked up to her. As though on cue, she and Daniel snatched their hands away and hid them under the table.

"Mr. Liu, how are you?" She half stood from her seat to receive his hug.

"Can't complain." His smile turned slightly guarded as he turned toward her dinner companion. "Hello, Daniel. Fancy meeting you here."

"Hello, Mr. Liu," Daniel replied, a look of polite indifference settling on his features.

With a bemused grunt, Walter Liu raised his eyebrows at her in obvious question of her choice for company.

"My father was supposed to join us, but he got detained at work," she explained.

"Minsung works too hard." Mr. Liu clucked his tongue. "Well, enjoy your dinner, my dear. I better head back to my table before my wife sends out a search party."

"It was lovely seeing you," Megan said with genuine warmth. "I'll come by to say hello to Mrs. Liu in a bit."

Daniel waited until Mr. Liu was out of hearing range before he asked, "Do you have every member of the board wrapped around your little finger? Or is it just Walter Liu?"

"Not *every* member," she said with a teasing smile. She liked it when his wry humor snuck past his solemn demeanor. "Many of the board members are old family friends. They watched me and my sisters grow up, so they're kind of like uncles and aunties to us. They were a godsend when my mom…"

"I'm glad you and your family had good friends to support you when your mother passed away." His voice was gentle with compassion.

"Yeah, it helped a lot." Megan took a sip of water to soothe the constriction in her throat. "Especially for my father. I don't know what we would've done if it weren't for Walter Liu and Anne Werner. They were the only ones who could get through to him."

They were sitting in companionable silence when Megan gasped, her hand flying to her mouth.

"What's wrong?" His eyes darted over her face. "Are you okay?"

"Yes, I'm fine," she said, waving away his concern. "I know what we have to do."

"What do we have to do?" he asked warily.

"We both agree that we can't tell my father about our baby yet." She waited for her words to register with Daniel. "But we also agree that we can't keep this…situation between us a secret forever."

"No, absolutely not." He pinched the bridge of his nose. "Mr. Han has a right to know. We have to tell him as soon as we can."

"Right." She nodded curtly, impatient to share her brilliant plan. "So I know what we have to do to allow us to tell my father everything without getting you fired. And I'm not talking about waiting until the baby is born."

"I'm listening." He didn't sound too hopeful. *O ye of little faith.*

"My father heeds the counsel of his friends, Walter and Anne, who also happen to be board members of Jigu Corporation." She gripped her hands together on her lap because she was waving them around too much. She always did that when she got excited. "From what I've seen, neither of them seems to be a huge fan of you."

"Harsh—" he cringed "—but fair."

"Sorry. But that's not the point. Well, that's kind of the point." She shook her head. "The *real* point is that we have to get Walter Liu and Anne Werner to bring you into their fold. As well as anyone else you think is still on the fence about you."

"I plan to earn their trust, but that's going to take

some time," Daniel said. "Once they see what I'm doing for Jigu Corporation as its CFO, they'll come around eventually."

"No, we don't have time to wait for them to *come around eventually*." She gave an impatient shake of her head.

"Then, what—"

She cut him off and blurted, "I can help you become a part of the *in* crowd."

"You're going to make me popular?" Amusement sparkled in his eyes.

"Ha-ha. I'm serious," she said, fighting back a smile. "Walter and Anne have a soft spot for me and my sisters. I can accompany you to some social events to show them you have the Han family stamp of approval and get them to warm up to you. Plus, I know them well so I can coach you on their likes and dislikes."

"And you're hoping that it'll be enough to compel them to hold your father back as he tries to choke the life out of me." He adjusted his tie as though he could feel it tightening around his neck.

"At the very least, they'll be able to convince him that it's not in Jigu's best interest to fire you," she said. "I mean, you're good at your job, right?"

"Damn right, I'm good at my job."

"Hmm." She tapped her index finger on her lips. "Maybe we should start by working on some humility."

Something close to a full-blown smile spread across

his face. Before she could become completely mesmerized by it, he said, "Are you sure your plan will work?"

"Have you got any better ideas?" She crossed her arms over her chest.

"If all else fails, there's always good old-fashioned groveling." His expression turned serious, and she wanted to whimper at the loss of his rare smile. "I'll do anything to be a part of our child's life."

Her heart puddled in her chest and renewed determination filled her. "My plan will work. I'll make sure of it."

Daniel knew he should slow down, but he didn't want to be late for Megan's prenatal appointment. He blew out a long breath and adjusted his grip on the steering wheel—his palms damp and slippery. He wouldn't be much use for moral support if he was a nervous wreck, so he shied away from thinking about the ultrasound and discovering the baby's sex.

Did all newly expectant parents feel like they were venturing into the jungle with their eyes blindfolded? *Hell.* It would probably help to admit that he had no idea what he was doing and accept that he would have to learn everything along the way. All he could do at this point was be there for Megan in whatever way she needed him.

He spotted Megan on a bench right outside the medical building. He quickened his pace just as she glanced up and smiled at him. The late-afternoon sunlight shone down on her upturned face and his breath got lodged in his throat.

"Am I late?" He hoped she didn't notice how husky he sounded.

"No, I'm early. We still have five minutes till the appointment," she said, getting to her feet. He hastily reached for her elbow to help her up even though she had no trouble standing on her own. She smirked but humored him. "Thank you."

After checking in, Megan pointed him toward the warm, pink waiting room and disappeared behind a door, saying something about peeing in a cup. Daniel couldn't help gawking a little at the other patients in various stages of their pregnancy. He was still standing where she'd left him when Megan came back to his side. She touched his arm and led them to a set of chairs.

"It's pretty wild, huh?" She placed her hand on the soft curve of her belly. "I'm barely starting to show, but soon I'm going to look like I swallowed a watermelon whole."

A smile tugged at his lips and he gave in to it. "I think all of you in here are heroes—incredibly brave and beautiful."

"I know. We are freaking sacred vessels." Although her words were playful, her voice held a hint of awe. "I still can't believe I'm growing a teeny-tiny human being inside me."

A teeny-tiny human being that was part him and part her. He coughed into his fist and shifted in his seat. None of this felt truly real to him, but he was certain it was going to hit him hard sometime soon.

"Megan Han?" A nurse in purple scrubs called from a doorway.

"Yes," Daniel answered at the same time as Megan, then felt like a fool.

"Come this way," the nurse said with a kind smile.

They were shown to a room, then told that the doctor would be with them shortly. Megan perched herself on the end of the examination table. The room was quite small, so Daniel stood close by her side.

A tall brunette in her early thirties walked into the room after a quick knock. "Hi, Megan. How are you feeling today?"

"Like a million bucks now that the morning sickness is gone," Megan said. "Dr. Pinkus, this is Daniel."

"Nice to meet you, Daniel." She pulled on a pair of latex gloves. "So this is the first baby for the two of you, right?"

The question seemed directed at him, so he managed a nod.

"How lovely. Well, this is going to be an extra-special appointment." She smiled brightly at them. "Megan, why don't you lie down and get comfortable? Then we'll get started with the ultrasound."

Dr. Pinkus tucked some paper towels into the top of Megan's leggings and tugged them lower with care, then lifted her shirt to just under her breasts. Daniel forced himself to look away from the sight of her bare midriff but not before he remembered the sound of her breathless laugh as he trailed his lips down to her belly button. He jerked his thoughts back to the present.

"We've warmed this up for you," the doctor said as

she squeezed a dollop of clear gel on Megan's stomach. "Here we go."

The sound that soon filled the room reminded Daniel of a steam locomotive speeding down the track.

Megan glanced at him and whispered, "That's the baby's heartbeat."

"All right," Dr. Pinkus said, "and here is your baby. Ten fingers. Ten toes…"

Daniel felt the tips of Megan's fingers brush against his palm. He grabbed hold of her hand and held on tight. At first glance, the black-and-white image on the screen looked like random smudges, until he saw the outline of a baby. His chest constricted and his eyes burned with unshed tears.

He finally looked away from the screen when he heard Megan's choked sob. Tears were streaming down her cheeks, past her smiling lips. He used his free hand to brush back her long hair from her face.

"It's a boy," the doctor said in a gentle voice. "And he is healthy and developing nicely."

"Oh, Daniel." Megan squeezed his hand. "We're having a son."

His son. He didn't trust his voice, so he leaned down and kissed her forehead, letting his lips linger against her soft skin. Such easy affection was out of character for him, but it felt so natural with Megan that it almost felt wrong not to touch her. He didn't give a damn if he was stepping on some coparenting partnership line. Not right now.

"When you're ready, you can pick up the ultrasound pictures at checkout." Dr. Pinkus wiped the gel off Megan's stomach. "I'll see you in four weeks."

"Thank you, Doctor." Daniel finally managed to form words.

He turned away as Megan sat up and adjusted her clothes. His protective instinct tried to overwhelm him as the reality of her pregnancy sank in and took root. If he had his way, he would carry her down to her car. Instead, he took a deep breath and linked his fingers through hers as they walked out of the examination room.

When they arrived at her car, he reluctantly released her hand. "If it isn't too much trouble, could you text me the pictures of the ultrasound?"

Megan's eyebrows sprang up in surprise before a lovely smile blossomed on her face. "It won't be any trouble. I'll send them to you as soon as I get home."

"Thank you." He caught himself staring at her, so he took a quick step back and stuck his hands in his pockets. "I should get back to the office."

"Wait—" she said and grabbed his arm. Blushing furiously, she quickly let go and straightened his sleeve. "I was thinking… Maybe we should attend the Breast Cancer Society's annual charity ball at the end of the month. Anne has been an active member in the group ever since my mom was diagnosed. At any rate, it would be a good opportunity for you to earn some brownie points with her. And—"

"Yes," Daniel said a little louder than he'd intended.

"Oh." Megan blinked. "Okay."

He had no idea when exactly the ball was and

whether he had a scheduling conflict. He would cancel or reschedule whatever he had planned. Anything to see her sooner than at her next prenatal appointment four weeks later. He didn't question his desire to be with Megan. It wasn't romantically motivated. She was carrying his child. It was his protective instincts flaring again.

"I'll pick you up—" he began.

"No," she interrupted. "We should go separately. I don't want to give my father any encouragement about setting us up."

"Right." He recalled how adamant Megan was about not marrying him. He pushed aside the black mood threatening to overtake him. "I'll meet you there, then."

He should say goodbye and head to his car, but he stood rooted in front of her. She worried her bottom lip for a second before pushing up to her toes to peck him on his cheek. He sucked in a sharp breath from both the surprise and the heat that shot down to his groin. He somehow hung on to his control and didn't crush his lips against hers.

"Thank you for coming today," she said with an endearing shyness. "I'm so glad our baby—our son—has both of us in his life."

"Me, too," he croaked as desire and tenderness whirled inside him. "Thank you for including me in this journey."

In Megan's presence, Daniel became a man he hardly recognized as himself. The emotions she inspired in him made him feel as powerful as a towering mountain and as vulnerable as a leaf hanging on to a branch through a storm. His survival instincts told him to run, but he was afraid that he would find himself running toward her.

Four

Her sisters sat down on either side of her as the morning sunlight poured into the practice room. Megan was euphoric after yesterday's ultrasound and she couldn't wait to tell her sisters she was pregnant. But they were bound to worry about her single-mom status, so she had to figure out a way to break the news to them gently.

"Which piece should we start with today?" Angie asked, thumbing through her sheet-music folder. "How about the *String Trio Op. 3*?"

"It's too early in the morning for—" Chloe yawned loudly "—Beethoven."

Her older sister gasped with exaggerated outrage. "It is never too early for Beethoven."

"I'm pregnant," Megan blurted, interrupting their

argument. That might not have been the gentlest way to tell them, but she couldn't hold it in a second longer. At least she refrained from stepping onto her chair and singing the words at the top of her lungs.

The silence in the room was eerie. For three whole seconds.

"Oh my God. I'm going to be an auntie," Chloe shrieked, her feet tapping the ground as though her shoes were trying to run away from her. "Wait. Is it okay for me to be happy about it?"

"That depends." Angie angled her body toward Megan. "Are *you* happy about it?"

"I'm so happy." Megan promptly burst into tears. Her older sister wrapped Megan in her arms, and her younger sister patted her head. She hiccupped once and said, "I didn't plan for this to happen, but I feel so blessed."

"Then, we are very happy for you," Angie said, squeezing her tightly against her. "Oh, my goodness. A baby. I can't believe it."

When Megan sat up to blow her nose, she saw her sisters exchange a speaking glance—they wanted to know *everything*. She braced herself to be bombarded with questions.

"Have you been seeing someone in secret?" Chloe nudged Megan with her shoulder.

"No… I met someone after last season's final performance. And…and…I slept with him—a total stranger—then snuck out of the hotel room in the middle of the night." Megan paused as Angie gasped and Chloe snorted. They knew she'd never had a one-night stand before. Her sisters quickly composed themselves and signaled for her to continue. "By the time I realized I was pregnant, I had no way of reaching him because I never asked for his phone number. We didn't even exchange our last names."

"So the baby's father has no idea you're pregnant?" Angie did an admirable job of keeping her voice even.

"No, he knows," Megan mumbled.

"How?" her sisters asked in unison.

"Do you want the short version or the long version?" Megan rummaged around her purse and pulled out a bag of Sour Patch Kids. She ripped open the bag and stuffed a handful of the gummy goodness into her mouth.

"Short," her sisters said together again.

"Then the long, unedited version right after," Chloe clarified.

"The short version? Jigu Corporation's new CFO, Daniel Pak, is the father of the baby," Megan said with a nervous cringe.

"What the literal hell?" Angie groaned. "Does Appa know?"

"No, he does not know." Megan held up her palms and shook her head. "And he absolutely cannot know. At least, not yet."

Her older sister massaged her temples. "You better give us the long version."

"Ooh, start from how you guys met." Chloe scooted to the edge of her seat.

Megan got the requisite ribbing when she revealed to her sisters that her car ran out of gas the night she

met Daniel, followed by plenty of disbelieving mur-
murs when she told them about their surprise reunion.
At the end, she relayed her dilemma about revealing
the baby's parentage to their dad and her plans to
solve the problem.

"You were one hundred percent right not to agree
to a loveless marriage," Angie said with a firm nod.
"Being a single mom will be hard, but you'll have me
and Chloe by your side."

"Daniel wants to be a part of the baby's life, too."
Megan's voice turned husky with sudden emotion.

Having Daniel at her prenatal appointment—
watching their baby on the screen with their fingers
linked—had felt deeply right to her. But whatever
she was beginning to feel for him had to stop now.
He'd made his opinions about love crystal clear that
night at the café. If she did something very foolish like
fall in love with him, then she was guaranteed to get
her heart broken. And that would make coparenting
the baby much more difficult—not to mention painful. It would be ideal if she and Daniel could become
friends. There was no law against coparenting partners being friends.

"It's a boy, by the way," she announced proudly.
Her sisters screamed in excitement, then took turns
hugging Megan.

"But I'm not sure about lying to Dad," Chloe said,
pulling on her lower lip.

"I don't like it either, but it won't be for long."
Megan whipped out the ultrasound picture. "Look at

this beautiful baby boy. We have to make sure that he has both a mother *and* a father in his life. Right?"

"Right." Her younger sister smiled and reached for the picture. "How cute is he? He looks like a gummy bear. No, wait. Oh my God. He's a Sour Patch Kid!"

"Let me see." Angie took the ultrasound from Chloe, then doubled over laughing. "Aww, look at our little Sour Patch Kid."

"Yes, it's funny because I eat a lot of Sour Patch Kids," Megan deadpanned. "You guys are hilarious."

"Let's call him SPK until you name him," Chloe cheered.

"We are not calling my child SPK." Megan snatched back the picture of her precious baby. "Don't worry, baby boy. Mommy will protect you from your aunties' mischief."

"You called yourself *mommy* so naturally." Angie covered her mouth with her hand, choking back a sob. "This is really happening. My baby sister is going to be a mom."

Tears streamed down Megan's cheeks once more. "Look what you've done, Unni. It's really hard to turn this off once it starts these days."

"Cry all you want." Her older sisters wiped Megan's face with a tissue. "We'll laugh and cry and celebrate this baby."

"I love you guys so much," Megan said, crying harder.

"We love you, too." Chloe sniffled.

Megan could stand on her own and face anything life threw at her. But it was so much better to do it with her sisters by her side—especially playing Beethoven in E-flat major at ten in the morning.

The ultrasound picture burned a hole in Megan's pocket as she sat down for dinner with her dad. On the one hand, she was dying to show off the image of her baby boy. She had to tell him soon anyway, and she knew he would love the child growing inside her once he digested the news. On the other hand, she didn't want to see the disappointment on her dad's face when she told him she was pregnant as a result of a one-night stand.

In a moment of weakness, she thought about telling him that she had been seeing someone, but it didn't work out. But she was already keeping the identity of the baby's father a secret from her dad and she couldn't handle any more lies. He really deserved better.

"Is everything okay?" her dad asked.

"Yeah. Of course everything's okay." She sat up straight, like she'd been caught doodling in class. "Why wouldn't everything be okay?"

"You've been pushing around that broccoli on your plate for the past five minutes." He leveled a stern glance at her. "Do I have to remind you to eat your vegetables?"

Megan laughed and popped the broccoli in her mouth. "I was just lost in thought."

"You and your sisters must be busy preparing for the upcoming season." Her dad took a guess as to her preoccupation.

"We are," she replied truthfully. "But we're excited to perform again."

"You know what you need?" He pointed his fork at her.

"No, Appa. What do I need?" She humored him with a wry smile.

"Golf." He nodded, agreeing enthusiastically with himself. "We should play a round on Saturday. It'll help you relax."

Her dad accepted the fact that none of his daughters would join the company he'd built—he accepted that they were born to be musicians. And it was what her mom had wanted and he would do anything for her. But he'd asked for one thing from her and her sisters. That they learn to play golf. He loved golf and wanted to share his passion with his daughters. She and her sisters had become competent golfers—Chloe was actually rather good—but Megan mostly enjoyed the conversations she shared with her dad on the green.

"It *has* been a while since we played a round," she said thoughtfully. They would talk and bond, then she would tell him she was pregnant. "It's a date."

Daniel stood outside the clubhouse, scrolling through some work email on his phone. Most could wait until Monday, but he would answer some later tonight. For now, he was determined to spend his Saturday like an actual weekend, playing a round of golf with Mr. Han. The familiar guilt that accompanied his thoughts about his mentor settled uncomfortably in his stomach. With a sigh, he pulled up the sonogram and traced the curved silhouette of the baby with the tip of his finger.

Keeping the truth from Mr. Han was in everyone's best interests, even though Daniel felt shitty about it. He couldn't risk being miles away from Megan and the baby, and Jigu Corporation needed him. Mr. Han would regret it if he fired Daniel in the heat of the moment. He was sure of that.

"I'm going to kill him," a melodic voice seethed from behind him.

He spun on his heels and came face-to-face with a furious Megan. "What are you doing here?"

"I can't believe he pulled this shit again," she railed, ignoring his question. "I told him he was embarrassing all of us."

He blew out a breath and rocked back on his heels. "So Mr. Han has struck again?"

"Yes." She paced back and forth in front of him with her fists on her hips.

Megan was obviously fuming, but she looked beautiful nonetheless. She wore a white sleeveless dress that flared around her hips, then fell inches shy of midthigh. Her ponytail bounced under her white cap as she continued to wear a groove on the pavement.

He glanced at his watch. "It's almost tee time."

She stopped and glanced quizzically at him.

"Well, it wasn't easy carving out the time to be here," he said, rubbing the back of his head. "And it would be a shame to waste such a beautiful day..."

He wasn't secretly glad that Megan had showed up instead of Mr. Han. And he definitely wasn't excited to spend the next several hours with her. There was no particular reason why his heart was racing.

"You're right." A rueful smile spread across Megan's face. "If you're anything like my father, I bet you rarely see the sunlight, being stuck in your office all day, every day."

"Guilty as charged." He raised his hand like a doofus, relieved she wasn't about to stomp straight off to go yell at her father.

"Can I make a confession? I actually don't enjoy golf very much. Don't tell my father. He'd be heartbroken if he found out. I only golf to spend time with him." Daniel felt himself deflate a little. *So much for spending a day in the sun with Megan.* But she continued, "Can I offer an alternative way to take advantage of this gorgeous day?"

"Please. Offer away." *Offer away?* He sounded like an eager pup.

"Why don't we go miniature golfing instead?" A mischievous light entered her eyes. "Maybe play a round of Skee-Ball? I'm a Skee-Ball *fiend.*"

"Skee-Ball?" His eyebrows drew together.

"Didn't your parents take you to arcades when you were little?" He was saved from answering—neither of them needed to have a conversation about his bleak childhood—because she went on to explain, "You roll this hard, heavy ball down a lane…"

"You mean like bowling?"

"No, no. There are no pins and the balls are baseball-sized." She cupped her hands to show him how big a baseball was since he obviously knew nothing. "Anyway, you roll the ball down a lane and into these small holes with different points. The harder to score, the higher the points."

"That sounds…fun?" He kept his face straight with some effort.

"Yes." Megan slapped his arm. "It is *the* best game in the world. Ooh, and we should definitely eat some greasy arcade pizza."

"Definitely." He gazed longingly at the clubhouse where they served the most delicious Monte Cristos. "Greasy pizza sounds fantastic."

"Oh, come on," she chided. "It's going to be fun. I promise."

"I'll hold you to it," he said, even though he would've happily watched paint dry with her. "Should we drive together? I'm not sure what we should do about your car…"

"No worries. My father had to go in to work this morning. He sent a car over to pick me up so he and I could drive home toge—" She gripped her forehead with her hand. "He deliberately left me stranded here so you'd have to give me a ride."

"How devious of him," Daniel said solemnly, biting the inside of his cheeks.

"I promise this won't happen again," she said with a pained expression.

He snuffed out the disappointment inside him. What was wrong with him?

Nothing good would come of indulging Mr. Han's matchmaking efforts. The longer they let it go on and got his hopes up, the more disappointed and betrayed his mentor would feel when he found out the truth—that Daniel and Megan had no intention of getting married even though he was the father of the baby.

And nothing good would come of indulging in his attraction to Megan. It would only complicate an already difficult situation. That was why they'd agreed to be coparenting partners and nothing more. His head understood that well enough, but his body was having a hard time remembering their agreement.

"It's not your fault." He dragged his fingers through his hair. "But it'll be wise to put an end to his matchmaking scheme soon."

"I was going to tell my father I'm pregnant after we golfed," she whispered, leaning close to him. "He won't keep pushing me on you if he thinks I'm pregnant with another man's child."

"Yes, you're probably right." The necessary omission twisted his gut with guilt, but it would only be until he won over key members of the board of directors. "How...? What will you tell him? About the baby's...father?"

"I'm going to stick as close to the truth as possible." She shrugged a bit helplessly. "I'll tell him I had a one-night stand with a stranger and that we parted without exchanging any contact information."

"I see," he murmured, more than a little concerned for Megan. It was the twenty-first century, but there was no denying that Korean-American culture remained rather conservative. Mr. Han was a good man, but he would no doubt be disappointed in his daughter. "Are you going to tell him tonight?"

"Yeah. There's no point in putting it off any longer."

"Will you be okay?" he asked even though he knew what her answer was going to be and that it would be a lie. She wasn't going to be okay. At least, not at first.

"Yes." She smiled tremulously, and a vise tightened around his chest. "I'll be fine."

"Well, we better fortify you for the showdown with some arcade pizza," he said, rubbing his hands together.

"And nachos. The processed cheese will coat me with a layer of protection."

He couldn't hold back his cringe. "Processed cheese. Of course."

Megan laughed and reached for her golf bag, but he snatched it away from her and hefted it onto his shoulder before pulling his own bag onto his other shoulder. "Shall we?"

They walked the short distance to his car, and Megan stood beside him typing into her phone as he loaded their golf clubs into the trunk.

"Okay," she said. "I found our place. Let's go."

Family Fun Palace was showing its age but was relatively clean, and the people who worked there seemed friendly and eager to help. The Western-themed miniature golf course was overrun by small kids, but their conscientious parents redirected them to focus on the game so the line didn't grow unbearably long.

Daniel didn't mind the short wait for the last hole as he watched Megan carefully jot down their score with a stubby pencil, munching on some Sour Patch Kids. She held out her hand and he dropped several more colorful pieces onto her palm. Her golf dress didn't have pockets, so he was the designated candy carrier. She plopped all of it into her mouth.

"We're tied," she mumbled morosely around a mouthful. "We can't end on a tie. This isn't freaking soccer."

"Who says I'm going to let you win?" He smirked and popped a piece of candy in his mouth. "Holy shit. What is in this stuff? It's disgusting."

"How dare you?" She snatched the nearly empty bag of Sour Patch Kids from his hand. "This is the single most perfect food in the world. And it was the only thing I could eat for the first trimester of my pregnancy."

"Then I'm grateful for its existence." Before he could stop himself, he reached out and ran his knuckles down her cheek. "I'm sorry. It sounds like you had a hard time."

"It was awful, but it's so worth it." She leaned into his touch before she pulled back suddenly. "Um, I think we're up."

Daniel cursed under his breath for acting on his impulse and followed Megan's brisk steps to the putting area. She stood back to let him set down his neon-green ball on the tee.

"Par nine," he read from the sign by the ninth hole, wanting to scatter the awkward air between them. He arched an eyebrow in challenge. "I'll do it in five strokes."

"Good luck with that," Megan said, crossing her arms over her chest. "Why don't we make this a bit more interesting? The loser buys the winner a slushy."

"You're on," he said, pointing his index finger at her. Never mind that he would not drink the blended colored water to save his life.

He maneuvered the ball for the final putt in three strokes. Megan stood beside him with her hand on her forehead. He couldn't remember the last time he'd had so much fun—quite possibly never. He turned to her with a shit-eating grin. "You must be tired. I don't see the point of you even taking your turn."

Megan held up a finger with a neatly trimmed nail painted in a deep, vibrant purple. But considering which finger she chose to raise, he didn't think it was meant for him to appreciate her edgy manicure. She dumped the last of the vile candy into her mouth and tossed the empty bag in the trash. Then she positioned her putter by her fluorescent pink ball. He shook his head. She was going to need at least three more strokes to finish. He should be a nice guy and give her the slushy she was going to buy for him.

Her putter met the ball with a sweet clang, and he watched with his mouth agape as her ball bounced and banked impossible curves and edges.

"Oh my God." She jumped up and down. "It's going in. *It's going in.*"

"No, no, no." He prayed for the ball to lose momentum, but it kept rolling and rolling, straight into the hole.

Megan screamed and threw herself into his arms.

With a huff of startled laughter, he lifted her off the ground before holding her close to him, pressing his cheek against her hair. She slowly quietened in his embrace but made no move to step away. Her tantalizing sweetness teased his nose, and her warm, soft curves pressed against him. Daniel couldn't deny how much he had longed to hold her like this—ever since he found her again.

She leaned back just enough to meet his gaze and he felt himself falling into the depths of her soft, brown eyes. He swept a strand of hair behind her ear with an unsteady hand and lifted her chin with the crook of his finger. Their faces were mere inches apart—so close he could feel the heat of her breath against his lips. He had to taste her. There was a reason he shouldn't, but he couldn't remember what. The need to kiss her consumed him and nothing else mattered. He slowly lowered his head...

"Ektuse me!" said a ringing voice with a childish lisp. "I hit ball. Hit ball fast and go potty."

Megan pushed away from him so abruptly that she nearly stumbled. He steadied her by her arms, then promptly dropped his hands. "You all right?"

"Yes. Yup. Mmm-hmm." She nodded as though her answer wasn't clear enough.

"I'm so sorry." A woman who appeared to be the toddler's mom waved her hand. "Please take your time."

"No, we're all done here," Daniel said, picking up Megan's putter off the ground where she'd dropped it before she flew into his arms. "I got my butt handed to me."

"I think I'm going to get an extralarge cherry slushy. No. Half cherry, half cola," Megan mused. He sneaked a glance at her and she was all smiles again. "I hope you learned an important lesson today. Never go against a Han when a slushy is on the line."

"Yeah, sure. Feel free to steal the Sicilian's line," he said with a teasing grin.

"You recognize the line?" Her eyes widened with pleasure. "I didn't peg you for a fan of *The Princess Bride*."

"As you get to know me, you'll discover that I'm full of surprises." He blinked and turned to stare straight ahead. He had never uttered a cornier sentence in his entire life. More importantly, was he flirting with her?

"Looking forward to it," Megan murmured.

His gaze shot back to her, but she wasn't looking at him. Was she flirting back? Did he want her to? He felt so completely turned around that he didn't know his right from left anymore. This wasn't like him. He always knew what he wanted. He always chose his path with deliberate care. With Megan, he felt as though he was hurtling down a grassy hill on a sunlit day. He couldn't deny that it was fun and exhilarating, but he felt out of control and more than a little scared.

Megan was intoxicating and that made her dangerous. He had to rein in his emotions before they got out of hand. He had enough riding on their partnership without risking his heart on top of it.

Five

Megan sat down at the dining table, glancing warily at the place setting for two. Her dad had been taking his dinner in his study for the past three nights, since she told him that she'd gotten pregnant from a one-night stand. He was understandably angry and disappointed in her. She sighed and smoothed her napkin on her thighs. It probably had slipped Mrs. Chung's mind that he wouldn't be joining Megan for dinner.

She was reminded that nothing ever slipped their housekeeper extraordinaire's mind when her father walked into the dining room and joined her at the table. She'd always prided herself in being brave and bold, but she couldn't meet her dad's eyes. Other than thanking Mrs. Chung when she brought out their dinner, neither of them said a word to each other for a long while.

The rice and soup in front of her blurred as her eyes filled with tears, but she inhaled deeply through her nose to hold off the ugly crying. When her dad reached out and placed a piece of grilled fish on her rice, she lost her perilous grip on her emotions and a choked sob escaped from her.

"You need to eat well," he said gruffly.

"I'm so sorry, Appa." She finally met his eyes as tears slid down her cheeks.

Her dad nodded solemnly and said with quiet menace, "When I find the bastard who took advantage of you, I'll tear him apart limb by limb."

"No one took advantage of me," she insisted, alarm jolting through her. "It was my choice. This pregnancy is an unexpected outcome, but I love this baby so much, and…and…"

"Now you understand how much I love you." He squeezed her hand.

"I love you, too." Megan pushed back her chair and knelt by her dad's side, resting her head on his knees. "I know this isn't the way you envisioned becoming a grandpa."

"I'm an old man set in my ways, but I need to learn how to roll with the punches. I lost so much time with Angie being an obstinate fool. When Umma was diagnosed with breast cancer, I would have moved mountains to save her—and to protect you girls from the heartache—but there was nothing I can do. I let my fear of losing her consume me and I became an overbearing tyrant. I forced Angie to leave the love of her life. I thought I was protecting her… I thought I knew best." She raised her head to look at him, taking his hand in hers. He smoothed her hair away from her face with his free hand and said, "I'm not going to repeat that mistake with you…especially with the little rascal on his way."

"Rascal?" She crinkled her nose at him. "He's going to be a perfect angel baby just like I was."

Her dad snorted loud enough to startle her. "When you were two, you thought you could fly. Umma and I seriously considered tying you to a chair after an exceptionally adventurous day."

Umma. What would her mom think if she knew that Megan was keeping the identity of the baby's father a secret from her dad? Guilt threatened to strangle the relief she felt at having her dad finally forgive her.

"The baby and I… We're going to be happy," she said to reassure her dad as well as herself. "You don't have to worry."

"Oh, my dear girl. Parents never stop worrying." His chuckle sounded melancholy. "But yes, you and the baby will be happy. I'll do everything in my power to make sure of that."

She believed him. And if he knew Daniel was the father of her baby, he would do everything in his power to force them to get married. She couldn't let that happen. She had to keep him in the dark for now. This was the only way for all of them to be happy. But knowing the secrecy was necessary didn't do anything to ease her guilt. Her dad's love and acceptance made her feel much, much worse about lying to him.

She managed to keep her unease to herself through dinner, then excused herself. She paced the length of her bedroom while wringing her hands. When that did nothing to make her feel any better, she stopped and shook out her hands, arms and legs. It felt as though ants were crawling all over her body. She had never lied to her dad before. Not like this. She wasn't sure how long she could keep it up.

She wanted to talk to her sisters, but she couldn't involve them in this charade any more than she had to. They'd promised not to say anything to their dad until Megan was ready to tell him herself. Even so, they didn't feel too great about it. No, she couldn't burden them with her turmoil. But who else could she talk to?

The answer was obvious. Still, she hesitated. Not because she didn't want to talk to Daniel. She hesitated because she desperately *wanted* to. They had met all of five times. He was a virtual stranger. But he didn't feel like one. She trusted him in a way that was all but impossible to explain. And she wanted his understanding and solace more than anything. She wanted *him*.

She grabbed her phone off her nightstand and stood with her thumbs poised over the keyboard. He felt bound to her by duty. He was attracted to her, but he didn't want anything *real* with her other than to coparent their child together. Reaching out to him tonight would be emotional self-sabotage.

She nearly dropped her phone when it pinged with a message from Daniel.

How did your talk go with your father?

Was this a courtesy text? If he was really worried, why didn't he text her three nights ago after their miniature golfing adventures? By the time they parted ways that evening, he'd grown quiet and distant. She chalked it up to him being tired or preoccupied with work after spending a rare day away from the office. But in all honesty, she'd instinctively understood that he was reinforcing the do-not-cross line between them. So why was he texting her now?

While she studied his question from all sides, her phone lit up with a new message.

I don't mean to intrude but… I wanted to make sure you were okay.

The truth. She could just answer his question with the truth. There was no need to overthink it.

He didn't speak to me for three days. Tonight, he told me he loves me and that he would do anything to make sure the baby and I are happy. That breaks my heart more than anything. I pretty much made a mess of everything.

Ellipses immediately began scrolling across her screen. She waited, nibbling her bottom lip. His message popped up at last.

Can I see you tonight?

Her heart stuttered in her chest. God, she wanted to see him.

Tonight? Like right now?

She stared at her phone.

I can be at your place in twenty minutes.

She shook her head as she typed.

No, not here.

But she also didn't want to fall apart somewhere public. She tapped out her suggestion before she could regret it.

I'll come over to your place.

His place turned out to be in one of the high-rise condos in Downtown LA not far from Jigu Corporation headquarters. She valeted her car and was shown to the penthouse elevator. He must've already added her to his guest list because keys were turned and buttons pressed without delay. The ride up to the top floor was smooth and fast, and the doors slid open before she felt ready.

Daniel stood a few feet away from the elevator with his hands in his pockets. He was still in a pair of slacks and a dress shirt, but with the top couple buttons undone and his sleeves rolled past his elbows. He looked gorgeous as hell. But that wasn't what had her throwing herself into his arms. The undisguised concern and sympathy in his eyes crumbled her defenses, and she couldn't hold herself back any longer.

His strong arms circled around her and held her close. She burrowed her face into the crook of his neck and pressed herself against him. She would just stay like this for a minute. There was no need for her to fall apart in front of him. She would accept the support he offered with dignity.

"I'm here," he said simply, his warm breath ruffling the hair by her temple.

She wished he'd stayed silent. She wished his words hadn't melted her heart into a puddle.

"No fair," she managed to choke out before she burst into tears. She was making his shirt all soggy, but she couldn't stop crying. "Sorry. Pregnancy hormones."

"You don't need to blame the hormones." His chest expanded and contracted with a heavy sigh. "Anyone dealing with what you're going through would be having a good cry."

She leaned back to meet his eyes and sniffed loudly. "Please stop saying all the right things."

"I'm saying all the right things?" His eyebrows crested above the bridge of his nose. "I should blurt out the first thing that pops into my head more often."

She huffed a watery laugh and moved to step away from him. He was slow to drop his arms—his hands skimming down her back in a way that made her shiver. Her gaze skittered away from his.

"Nice place," she said, glancing around the foyer painted in muted burgundy and gray. "At least what I can see of it."

"Hell, sorry." He scratched the back of his head. "I

obviously don't have people over much. Let me show you to the living room."

She pressed her lips together to keep from smiling. She didn't know why she wanted to smile, honestly. *Who cares if he doesn't have people over often?* She certainly didn't. He could invite women to his place as often as he'd like. It wasn't like they were romantically involved or anything. Megan trudged after him. Suddenly, she didn't feel like smiling at all.

"Make yourself comfortable." Daniel held out his hand toward a dark brown sectional to one side of the large living room, then headed toward the open kitchen on the other end. "Would you like something to drink?"

"Sure." She lowered herself onto the sofa and brushed her hand over the soft leather. "Tea would be nice."

"Yes, of course."

She watched him wander around the kitchen opening a cupboard here and a drawer there. She decided to give him a break when he started cursing under his breath. "Why do I get the feeling you don't come here often either?"

"What?" He spun away from the refrigerator, closing the freezer door. She didn't question why he was looking for tea in the freezer. "I only moved in a few months ago. I honestly don't do much here other than catch a few hours of sleep most nights."

A small frown pinched her forehead. As she'd suspected, Daniel was as much of a workaholic as her dad. But at least her dad had a family to provide some balance to his life. The thought of Daniel being lonely made her heart ache a little.

"On second thought, I don't need any tea," she said, patting the seat beside her. "Come join me."

Daniel felt like an idiot as he sat down next to Megan. He couldn't even give her a cup of tea. But offering her what he had in his freezer instead—and explaining why he had so many cartons of different flavors of ice cream—would be much more mortifying.

"Do you have family back East?" she asked, tucking her legs up onto the couch.

He stiffened reflexively at her unexpected question, but forced himself to relax. "Just my father."

"So you're an only child." She didn't phrase it as a question, so he didn't offer a response. "I can't imagine life without my sisters."

"I got used to being alone. You can't miss something you never had," he said with a matter-of-fact shrug. His mother had left him and his father when he was so young that he didn't remember her at all. It was as if he'd never had a mother.

"I guess that's true." She rested her chin on top of one of her knees. "What about your father? Do you miss him?"

"We aren't...close." He shifted in his seat. The understatement almost felt like a lie, but he couldn't exactly tell her that his father wished he'd never had Daniel.

"I'm beginning to think it's a good thing you have

me and the baby in your life," she said in a voice so quiet he wondered if he'd misheard her. But his pounding heart and the slight tremor in his body assured him that he'd understood her correctly.

"I didn't realize I got to have you in my life, too." And why did he say that? She probably didn't mean anything by it. He should've laughed it off instead of hanging on to her words as though they were the only things keeping him afloat.

Her eyes widened and a deep blush rose to her face. He wanted to brush his lips across her cheekbones to see if her skin felt as hot as it looked. "Well, since the baby is inside of me right now, we…the baby and I…kind of come in a package? For the time being?"

"I'm glad you come as part of it all," he said huskily. A jolt of fear shot through him at how happy the package deal made him. They were having a child together, but she didn't plan on being with him. She would leave like the others. As a reminder to himself, he repeated, "For the time being."

She nodded absently and drew circles on the couch with the tip of her index finger. *Hell.* What was he doing? He'd asked to see her so he could comfort her. The last three days must have been tough for her.

"I'm sorry your father took the news of your pregnancy so hard." He gently picked up her hand. "Was he very angry with you?"

"Very." Her sad smile felt like a punch in the gut. "But I expected that. And when he was angry with me, I felt a bit indignant and self-righteous. I thought to myself 'I'm a grown woman and I can do whatever the hell I want with my body.' The hard part—"

He squeezed her hand when she paused to swallow the emotion swelling up in her.

"The hard part came when he offered me his love and support, because I couldn't hide from the truth anymore. He was only angry because he was worried and scared for me. I can't believe I put him through that." She scoffed and shook her head. "I can't believe what I'm about to put him through by lying to him about who the baby's father is."

"It's not too late to tell him the truth." He gulped. Getting fired from Jigu Corporation was the last thing he wanted, but he couldn't bear to watch Megan hurting. "We could tell him together."

"Daniel, my father respects and trusts you, but if we tell him now that you are the baby's father and we refuse to get married, then he will fire you. My father is a relic from the Joseon Dynasty, when it comes to duty and honor. In the heat of the moment, he would think firing you is the only way to protect our family's honor—my honor." She took a deep breath and squared her shoulders. "His pride and temper often get the best of him, but once he comes to his senses, he'll regret losing you. I can't let him make that mistake. And it's not fair to you or our baby. We have no choice but to carry out our plan."

"I understand." He nodded. She was right, of course. "Is there anything I could do in the meantime to ease your burden?"

"No. Not unless you have ice cream," she said with a wistful smile.

He groaned and placed his head in his hands.

"What's wrong?" She scooted close to him and put her hand on his shoulder.

"What flavor do you want?" he growled.

"What? Oh…" She laughed. "I was just kidding. You don't need to conjure any up for me."

"Just…" He huffed and sat up straight. "Just humor me. Tell me what flavor you want."

"Um, cherry vanilla?" she said hesitantly.

"What else?" He wearily pushed himself off the sofa.

"Butter pecan?" She cocked her head to the side and regarded him curiously. "Are you seriously going out to get me ice cream right now?"

He stomped to the freezer without answering and grabbed a pint each of cherry vanilla and butter pecan. He pulled open a few drawers until he found a spoon and returned to the sofa.

"Ice cream," he announced unnecessarily and plunked down the cartons on the coffee table.

Megan's jaw dropped, and the shock on her face made him feel a little better. "How did you know I was going to ask for these flavors? Wait, how did you even know to have ice cream handy in your freezer?"

He sighed and sat back down on the couch. He might as well get this over with. "Do you remember how I volunteered to deliver whatever food you were craving?"

"Yes…"

"You mentioned that you might crave ice cream one of these days, but I had no idea what kind you like, so I bought one of virtually every flavor out there." His words ran over each other in his rush to get them out. "I like to be prepared. I didn't want to go jumping from store to store, searching for a particular variety of ice cream. Who wants to keep a pregnant woman waiting? A damn fool. That's who."

He stopped talking because he knew he was rambling like a...damn fool. He thought Megan would be rolling around the floor laughing by now, but she didn't make a peep. He finally turned to glance at her. The tenderness in her expression nearly undid him.

"You did all that for me?" she whispered.

He reached out and ran the back of his hand down her cheek. "I wanted to do something for you... anything. I can't even imagine everything you're going through. How can I help? What can I do?"

She leaned into his touch, cupping her hand over his. "This. I think everything you've done tonight is exactly what I needed."

He couldn't look away from her. She was so close and so beautiful. He felt his head tilting toward her. He couldn't stop himself, but he moved as slowly as he could so she would have a chance to turn away from him. She didn't turn away. Her mouth parted on a shaky breath and her eyes tugged him closer yet.

It was barely a touch—a brush of parted lips against parted lips—but his world seemed to stop. He drew back only enough to search her face, but she gasped with outrage and promptly brought his lips back on hers with her hands buried in his hair. With a helpless, desperate groan, he kissed her the way he'd been starving to kiss her.

He nipped at her full bottom lip, then licked it. He tilted his head to one side, then the other, tasting her from all angles. When she moaned, he plunged his tongue into her hot mouth and wrapped his hand around the back of her neck, steading her against his onslaught. She pushed closer to him, her breasts pressed against his chest. It wasn't close enough.

Daniel leaned back on the sofa until Megan was lying on top of him, kissing him as though she couldn't get enough of him either. Straddling his waist, she sat up long enough to tear her shirt off, then he dragged her back as though kissing her was the only way he could breathe. Their lips moved against each other's, wild and clumsy.

His erection strained against his trousers and he hooked his thumbs into the top of her pants, tugging impatiently. She sucked in a surprised breath and scrambled off him. He rose onto his elbows to find her sitting with her knees drawn to her chest on the other end of the couch. Bewildered, he sat up and clawed his hands through his hair. Shit. He'd gotten so caught up in his desire, he must have pushed her too fast.

"Megan, I'm sorry," he panted, trying to catch his breath.

"No. No, don't be." Her chest was still heaving. "I just…"

"You don't need to explain." He held up his hand.

"Shit. I shouldn't have done that. We had an agreement and you're vulnerable right now. I crossed the line—"

"Just shut up and listen for a minute," she commanded. He snapped his mouth shut. She took a deep breath and continued, "I'm wearing maternity pants."

"Why does…? Pardon?"

"When you tugged on my pants, I realized I was wearing maternity garb." She stretched her legs out so he could see them more fully. "It has this stretchy, elastic panel and…it's not very sexy."

His eyes dropped to her waistline and he noticed the soft curve of her stomach for the first time. Emotion rose up to his throat and heat spread through his chest. She was so beautiful. Then a thought made his blood drain from his face. "Oh God. Did I hurt you? The baby—"

"Stop it. I'm fine. We're fine." She buried her face in her hands. "I'm just embarrassed. Okay? It's like getting caught on a date wearing a pair of granny underwear."

Incredulous laughter huffed out of him.

"Are you laughing at me?" Megan's eyes narrowed dangerously.

"I happen to value my life." He grinned and picked up her top from the ground. He pulled it carefully over her head and helped her slide her arms in. He smoothed down her shirt and placed both his hands on her shoulders. "You don't have any idea how beautiful you are, do you?"

"Who looks beautiful in maternity pants?" She turned her head to the side.

He gently grasped her chin between his fingers and made her look at him again. "You."

She stared at him as though she wanted to call his bullshit. He held her gaze because he meant what he said and he wanted her to know that. A soft blush stole across her face. Her eyelashes fluttered and she smiled shyly at him.

"Sorry for halting things so abruptly," she said at last.

"It's for the best." He didn't necessarily believe that at the moment, but he should. Megan was guilt ridden enough without adding another thing to hide from her father. And he knew better than to touch the CEO's daughter when things were quite tangled up as it was. Too bad his intelligence became questionable every time he was around this woman. "We shouldn't do anything we might regret. Coparenting partners, remember?"

Some of the light left Megan's eyes and he wanted to take back his words. But it was for the best. If he told that to himself enough times, he might even believe it.

"Oh, the ice cream," she said, reaching for a carton. "I almost forgot."

"I can get you some different ones if those melted."

"No, they're still good. I like mine a little runny." She scooped up a generous mound of cherry vanilla and licked it off the spoon. "Mmm."

"Happy?" he asked as euphoria filled her face.

"Happy," she said around another mouthful.

"Good." He leaned back on the couch and quietly watched her decimate two cartons of ice cream.

This had to be enough. He would provide her with ice cream, accompany her to her prenatal appointments and offer his support when things got difficult for her at home. If he didn't get greedy, this might be enough for him. It had to be.

Six

Megan's favorite part about the Breast Cancer Society's annual fundraising ball was its venue at the Ebell of Los Angeles clubhouse. The historic two-story building was constructed nearly a hundred years ago in the Italian Renaissance style with a smooth white exterior and dark clay-tile roofing. The dining hall, where the main event would be held, boasted high engraved ceilings and stately columns. With rich wood panels and wrought-iron railings, it felt like a place from another time.

But what made the place truly magical for Megan was the tiled-roof colonnade that led to the mani-cured courtyard garden. The walkway arches sur-rounded two sides of the space, draped with silky fuchsia curtains to complement the pink theme, which commemorated the fight against breast cancer. Intricate topiaries lined the street-facing side so the guests could forget that they were idling in a building by a busy Los Angeles street.

Cocktail hour was well underway in the picturesque garden, and guests in tasteful formal wear milled about the ornate water fountain aglow with ambient lighting. Megan walked over to the bar set up in the corner and ordered a club soda with lime. Her Grecian, empire-waist gown effortlessly hid her baby bump, but there was no reason to announce that she wasn't drinking.

"Thank you." She took the glass the bartender extended to her and opened her clutch.

A long arm reached around her and placed a couple twenties in the tip jar. "I'll have the same."

"Daniel." Her voice sounded huskier than she'd like, but she couldn't stop her heart from fluttering at the sight of him. He looked magnificent in a classic tuxedo, fitted to show off his athletic physique to perfection. He wore his hair slicked back from his forehead, adding an irresistible air of sophistication. "You made it."

With his drink in one hand, he placed his other on the small of her back and led her toward one of the draped arches. "Of course. I've been looking forward to it."

"Looking forward to the ball? Or looking forward to seeing me?" She smiled up at him from beneath her lashes.

"I, uh…" He cleared his throat and recovered admirably. "Both. I was looking forward to both."

They hadn't met since the night at his penthouse. He had texted periodically to check in on her but they were more polite than anything else. She wanted to scream with frustration every time she got one, but she sent an equally polite response back. She was biding her time to make her move. And yes…she had every intention of making a move.

Something had shifted for her that night Daniel offered her ice cream in any flavor she could possibly want. His gruff tenderness and vulnerability moved her to the core, and she wanted him. It was foolish and inconvenient. He made it clear that he would regret getting involved with her. Maybe he was right. Maybe they would be sorry. She would loathe having yet another secret to keep from her father. But Megan knew she would regret it more if she didn't at least try to explore the attraction between them. It was something rare and special—at least for her.

"Good answer," she said. "Shall we go find Anne and get you those brownie points?"

"By all means. Lead the way." His hand found its way back to the curve of her back, and shivers of awareness skipped down her spine. "We aren't going to run into your father here, are we?"

"No, it's hard for him to attend these events. Even after seven years, my mom's death is still a raw wound for him." She sighed. "I've been coming and donating on his behalf for the last several years, so we're safe to proceed with our plan."

Anne was in the dining room, adjusting the pink floral centerpieces and smoothing out the bows on the satin chair covers. She looked impeccably elegant in an emerald A-line gown, but a small frown marred her forehead.

"Everything looks absolutely perfect." Megan leaned down to kiss the older woman's cheek. "You can stop fussing."

"Tim stepped out to the garden to get a drink." Anne laughed and rotated the centerpiece by a quarter turn. "He said I was making him nervous."

Megan wrapped her arm around Anne's shoulders and turned them both to face Daniel. "Look who I found wandering about."

"It's good to see you, Mrs. Werner." His words were friendly enough, but his expression was aloof as he extended his hand toward her. That wouldn't do.

Megan cleared her throat softly. His eyes flitted toward her and she mouthed "Smile," pantomiming a toothy grin.

"Thank you, Mr. Pak." Anne placed her hand in Daniel's with a regal nod. "I'm so glad you could make it."

"You've done an amazing job. The event looks like a success," he said with a hint of a smile. That was better. "And please call me Daniel."

Anne made a noncommittal noise and said, "I didn't realize you two knew each other."

"He came over for dinner one evening and we kind of hit it off," Megan explained. "Call us golfing buddies. We mostly complain about my father to each other."

He held out his hand and hurriedly averred, "I have the greatest respect for Mr. Han."

"Of course you do. We both do. Great man, my father." Megan winked at him and whispered to Anne, "As an added bonus, Daniel is very fun to tease."

"Megan, do be gentle with him." Anne smiled sympathetically at Daniel. "You have to watch out for this one."

"I appreciate the heads-up," he said, his grin widening. "I'll be sure to stay on my toes."

"Look at you two…ganging up on me." Megan was delighted that Daniel had relaxed enough to let some of his charm shine through.

"We have to even out the playing field somehow," he said, still wearing that beautiful smile. He turned to Anne with humor twinkling in his eyes. "I'll come find you if I need reinforcement."

The older woman laughed, genuine warmth stealing into her expression. "I'll be on the lookout for you."

"Fine. Be that way." Megan wrinkled her nose at them.

"Well, we'll leave you to prepare." Daniel raised his drink and said, "Here's to record-breaking donations."

"Thank you, Daniel. Fingers crossed," Anne said with another fond smile. Then she pulled Megan over to the side and whispered, "Some men look like they were born to wear a tuxedo. Have fun *playing golf* with him."

"Miss Anne," Megan gasped. "We're just friends."

"Whatever you say." Anne wiggled her eyebrows.

Megan cast a quick glance at Daniel, who appeared to be studying the tastefully decorated dining room with interest. "I had to nip my dad's matchmaking fantasies in the bud, so don't you start now."

"Oh, I don't know. You know what they say about the wisdom of elders…"

"I'm going back out to the beautiful garden to enjoy the evening with my *friend*."

Megan hurried off before Anne could continue her teasing. But it was a good sign that she was trying to play matchmaker, too. Her dear friend had taken a liking to Daniel. Now it was up to him to keep the rapport alive.

"Hey, shall we go mingle?" she said, coming to stand next to him.

"Must we?" he drawled dryly. He glanced toward the throng outside with a faint grimace and sipped his drink.

"What?" She widened her eyes innocently. "You don't enjoy smiling until your cheeks cramp, while making small talk with virtual strangers who listen to you with half an ear and silently judge you?"

"It's so delightful. How could I not enjoy that?" He chuckled, the warm sound making her toes curl. She had to try to make him do that more often.

She hooked her arm through his and strolled onto the walkway that led to the garden. "If you pretend that all the people are gone, there's a quiet beauty to this place."

"Maybe we should hide somewhere to enjoy it." He glanced sideways at her and let his eyes linger until her skin tingled as though he'd run his hands down her body. He wanted her as much as she wanted him.

"There may be an alcove at the end of this walkway," she murmured and slowly sashayed her way past the crowd.

The time was ripe to make her move.

The sway of Megan's hips mesmerized him as she glided down the walkway ahead of him. He caught up with her in three long strides and placed his hand on her lower back, his bottom two fingers pressed tantalizingly close to the curve of her ass. His nostrils flared as he caught a whiff of her sweet, floral scent, and reason slipped out of his mind.

He had been determined to keep his distance since the night she came over to his place. He didn't want to betray Mr. Han's trust further by sleeping with his daughter behind his back. And it wouldn't be easy for Megan to keep another secret from her father. The last thing he wanted was to add to her already full plate. But when he saw her standing in the garden tonight— a vision in her flowing red dress—he knew he would crawl through burning coal to have her again.

She reached for his hand, and he threaded his fingers through hers, and she pulled them into a shadowy alcove and pressed her back against the wall. He placed his hands on either side of her head and stared at her face until his eyes adjusted to the dark. He sucked in a sharp breath when she slid her palms over his chest and wrapped her arms around his neck.

"I don't want to burden you with another secret to

keep from your father." He held himself in check even as desire pumped through his veins.

"I think fighting this attraction between us is the bigger burden," she whispered. His head dipped toward her of its own volition, and she wet her lips. "What are you doing, Daniel?"

"Surviving," he said, his voice a low growl. "Because I can't live through another night without having you."

She smiled then—a sensual, triumphant smile— and he was lost. He crushed his lips against hers with a groan and she immediately opened up for him. He plunged his tongue into her mouth again and again, drawing a moan from her. She pressed her body against his, molding his hardness against the softness of her stomach. His hips jerked helplessly as his fingers dug into her hips, pulling her even closer to him.

He cupped her breast over her dress and trailed hot, wet kisses down the column of her neck. Hooking his finger onto her shoulder strap, he tugged it down to reveal more skin for him to taste. His lips dipped to the curve of her breast, flowing above the low-cut bodice. She thrust her chest into his face, rising on her tiptoes. With an impatient growl, he tugged on her bodice because he wanted more…needed more. But the sound of ripping fabric stopped him short.

"Don't stop," she panted when he raised his head and tried to tug him back.

"God, Megan. If we don't stop now, I might take you against this wall." He kissed her hard so she could taste his desperation but pulled back before he lost control again.

"That'll give this fundraising ball a whole new kind of vibe, because I won't be able to keep quiet." She pressed her forehead against his and let out a huff of frustrated laughter. "By the way, did you rip my dress?"

"I might've gotten a little carried away." He grimaced as he slid her shoulder strap back in place. This was so unlike him. He wasn't the type who ripped women's clothes off in a rush to get them naked. He respected buttons and zippers. "I don't think I did too much damage."

"The tear is right under my arm." Megan looked down at her bodice and adjusted it. "As long as I don't wave my arms around, it shouldn't be that visible. It's a good thing tonight isn't a bachelor auction."

His forehead creased with a frown. "Would you be that eager to bid on an eligible bachelor?"

"Well, I *am* a sucker for a burly firefighter." Her eyes twinkled merrily as she teased him.

"Oh?" He arched his eyebrow, not at all amused. "Not into cowboys, are you?"

"Truth be told, I'm sort of into the introverted corporate-executive type." She gave him a sweet peck on the cheek—and wrapped him around her pinkie finger. He bit the inside of his mouth to stop himself from grinning like an idiot.

"I think they're announcing dinner." He frowned as a thought occurred to him. "Will we be seated at different tables since we came separately?"

"Don't worry. I have a feeling Anne made some adjustments on the seating chart to have us sit next to each other."

"I'll have to thank her for that," he murmured as they joined the throng entering the dining room.

"Nothing says thank-you like a big, fat donation," Megan advised. "She'll adore you for that."

"Wouldn't that be buying her approval?" He'd intended to make a generous donation—the fact that breast cancer took Megan's mother away from her made the cause feel much more personal—but he didn't want to use it as a way to get close to Anne.

"Not in the way you think. It won't be the money but your willingness to donate to a good cause—your good deed—that will win you her appreciation."

"This definitely is a worthy cause." He hesitated for a beat, then said, "And I know it was years ago, but I'm sorry about your mother."

"Thank you." The surprise and warmth in her eyes made him glad he'd said something. "We loved her very much, and it was devastating to lose her."

When they reached their table, he helped her into her seat, then sat down next to her. He reached for her hand under the table because he needed to touch her, and smoothed his thumb across her knuckles. He watched as a soft blush stole across her cheeks.

"This dinner is going to feel like an eternity," she said in a low voice.

"I'll be right here with you, slowly going mad, until I can take you home."

"And what are you going to do after you take me home with you?"

"Make you wish our night together will last an eternity." He drew small circles on the sensitive skin of her wrist, remembering how soft she was everywhere.

Tonight, when he had her, he was going to explore every last inch of her and draw a map of her in his head. He didn't know how long he could have her, but he would guard every minute with her.

Seven

Megan could be impulsive, but she rarely regretted her actions. She was an intuitive person, and her intuition never steered her wrong...but there could always be a first time.

She fiddled with the tiny beading on her clutch as the elevator zoomed up to Daniel's place. They hadn't talked much on their drive over, and an odd, charged silence had settled between them. Considering their hot-as-hell kiss in the alcove and the hand orgy they engaged in under the banquet table, she thought they'd be tearing each other's clothes off in the elevator.

She jumped a little when the elevator dinged and the doors slid open onto the penthouse. Daniel held out his arm for her to proceed, so she strode down the hallway and into the living room. If she had been feeling ballsy, she would've walked straight into his bedroom—if she knew where it was—but she was so nervous, her legs bounced restlessly when she sat down on the couch.

Daniel didn't sit. He didn't say a word. He just paced the floor on the other side of the coffee table until she wanted to tackle him to make him stop. Or maybe to kiss him senseless. Apparently, she was capable of feeling both anxious and horny at the same time. Without pausing in his quest to meet his step goals, he loosened his bow tie and threw it on the armchair. His jacket followed suit. When he undid the button at his wrist and began rolling up his sleeve, she almost lost it. *What the hell?* Was this a forearm striptease? And was she expected to sit still and watch? Must. Touch. Forearms.

He finally stopped and knelt in front of her. "Megan, I want you."

"Thank God," she breathed. "I want you, too."

"But I can't… I can't give you what you need…" He ran his hand through his hair.

"You can't give me sex?" She sounded outraged even to her own ears.

"What?" He blinked. "I can give you sex. Shit. I mean I want to make love to you, but I can't give you some rose-tinted fantasy of love and happily-ever-after."

"Oh." A painful pang shot through her heart.

"I…care about you. You must know that," he said haltingly. "But love could consume you…and shatter you. It's not a risk I'd ever wish to take."

He'd told her what he thought about love the night he proposed to her. She already knew that he couldn't give her the kind of love she had always dreamed about. The kind of love her mom and dad had shared—like the love Angie and Joshua had—where they so thoroughly belonged to each other that they didn't know where one soul ended and the other started. Even though she'd known, she couldn't stop the disappointment sweeping through her.

"I don't want to hurt you." He cupped her face with a gentleness she yearned to soak up like sunlight.

Her eyes roamed over his kind, handsome face. He didn't know it, but he was capable of love. She felt it down to her core. Her intuition had never steered her wrong. But even if he could never love her, she wanted this. She wanted the passion, the intimacy, the closeness. She wanted to share those things with this man even if it couldn't be forever.

"I'm not asking you to give me the fantasy, Daniel," she said, turning her head to plant a kiss on his palm. "I want *you*. That's all."

"But—"

She pressed her fingers to his mouth. "I'm *desperate* for you. Maybe it's just lust. Maybe it's something I can get out of my system. Let's just take this day by day. No promises."

Daniel was torn. She could see it in his eyes. He wanted her, but he was a good man and he didn't want to break her heart. If she played it smart, both of them could get what they wanted without anyone getting hurt. All she had to do was not fall in love with him.

"Make love to me, Daniel." She replaced her fingers with her lips. "Please."

She felt the gentle pressure of his hands on her shoulders…pushing her away. Mortification spread like hot water being poured down her head. He didn't want her. Not enough to weather the potential storm. But before she could rush off, Daniel raised her to her feet by her hand and led her through his house. Confused, she tugged on her hand, but he held firm until they reached his bedroom.

The room was minimally furnished with a king-size bed in the center, with two low nightstands on each side and a tufted bench at the foot of the bed. The white-and-gray-color motif could have made the room feel stark, but it actually felt open and inviting.

"Sorry about the mess," Daniel said, gathering some documents and folders scattered on the bed.

When he stood uncertain, with his hands full, Megan walked fully into his bedroom and took the folders from him and placed them down on the bench. "Just focus on why you brought me to your room."

"Are you saying I should focus on undressing you?" The uncertainty melted away from him and a rakish grin spread across his face. "And tasting every last inch of you?"

A thousand butterflies took flight in her stomach. She was suddenly very warm, but she had the wherewithal not to fan her face with her hands. "Oh, I thought you brought me here to show me the stunning view of the city."

"I had an entirely different view in mind." He put

his arms around her waist and pressed her against his body.

She shivered when he kissed the side of her neck and inched down the zipper on her dress. Reassured of his intent—which she hoped was to fuck her senseless—she slid her hand over the outline of his desire. "I think I remember which view you're talking about. It's quite stunning in its own right."

His throaty chuckle turned into a groan when she gave him a firm squeeze. He trapped both her hands behind her back and stared down at her face. His expression was almost feral with lust and hunger. "You need to behave or this will be over much sooner than either of us want."

"Must I?" She ground her hips against him. "Misbehaving is so much more fun."

He finally caved and captured her lips in a searing kiss. *About damn time.* She wiggled until he freed her hands and went to work on his shirt buttons without breaking their kiss. She had never undressed a man so quickly in her life. She pushed off his shirt and brought her lips to the smooth skin of his chest to nip and lick as she pleased.

When she scraped her teeth over his nipple, he hissed and set her away from him. Her indignant huff turned into a gasp when he ripped her dress off in a single motion, going down to his knees. He helped her step out of the dress and her strappy gold heels until she stood in front of him clad in a black satin bra and matching bikini panties. Teeny-tiny, bikini-style panties worked well for her baby bump because they sat below the curve of her stomach. *Thank the Lord for that.* Daniel stared at her near-naked body with reverence—for just a moment—before he divested her of the scrap of black cloth.

She cried out at the first reverent touch of his open mouth on her—soft, hot and wet. He tilted his head back to meet her eyes before sticking two of his fingers into his mouth, then slowly pulling them out. He glided those fingers through her folds, to open her up, and licked her swollen bud—a flicker at first, then with long, laving strokes.

The quakes started deep inside her lower stomach and gathered at her clit. The pressure built higher and higher, drawing a deep, guttural moan from her. When he took her in his mouth and sucked, she broke with a scream as waves and waves of pleasure crashed into her.

Daniel was on his feet before she could crumble to the ground and picked her up in his arms. He laid her down gently on the bed and stood back to unbuckle his belt and slide the rest of his clothes off. Even limp and languid, her eyes devoured the sight of his naked body and she reached out for him as he joined her at her side.

"You're so beautiful," he whispered, running his hand along her body from her breast to her hip.

"So are you." She tugged on his head until his lips met hers.

The tenderness soon gave way to passion and she squirmed against him as their tongues tangled and their teeth clacked against each other. He dipped his head and drew the tip of her breast into his mouth, and her back arched off the bed. Heeding her silent demand, he slipped his hand between her thighs and plunged a finger inside her. She rode his hand shamelessly as he slid in a second finger.

"Oh God," she panted and reached for his erection. "Daniel. Please."

He groaned and pumped his hips into her fist. "What, baby? What do you want?"

"I want you inside of me." She swirled her thumb over the velvety skin of his tip.

"Fuck," he growled and jerked against her hand.

"Do you want me, too?" she asked with a knowing smile.

In response, he pinned her arms over her head and kissed her until she couldn't breathe. Then he spun around to grab a condom from his dresser and ripped open the packet.

"Wait," she said breathlessly. "Are you...STD free? Because I am. They do all these tests when you get pregnant—"

"Focus, Megan." His laughter rumbled in his chest, but there was desperation in his eyes. "I don't have any STDs..."

"Then, we don't need that." She nodded at the condom in his hand. "It's not like I can get pregnant again. And I want to feel you with nothing between us."

"God, yes."

She opened her legs and wrapped them loosely around his waist. His shoulders taut with control, he entered her with painstaking care, rocking in and out, inch by inch. With a feral growl, she dug her fingers into his ass, tilted her hips and pulled him inside her to the hilt. Her head rolled back and she shouted with satisfaction.

"Megan." Daniel froze over her. "Are you okay?"

"You…feel…so good inside me." She swiveled her hips. "Please take me. I'm not going to break. I want you to take me hard and fast. Please."

A choked groan escaped him before he started riding her with an intensity that took her breath away. It felt glorious. His measured thrusts soon lost their rhythm and he pounded mercilessly into her. She thought she was spent from her last orgasm, but she felt one building inside her again. Her head started rolling from side to side as she met him thrust for thrust.

"Daniel," she moaned as white stars exploded behind her lids, coming even harder than the first time.

He shouted as he reached his own climax and jerked inside her once, then twice. He held himself over her with trembling arms and kissed her hard on her lips before collapsing on the bed beside her. When she could move her limbs, she turned to her side and patted his rock-hard abs.

"Rest up, tiger." She yawned. "Because we're going to do that again."

When he shook with breathless laughter, she snuggled against his side and smiled lazily.

"I'm just going to close my eyes for a second,"

she said and drifted off to sleep, soothed by the feel of Daniel's hand stroking her naked back. It felt so good and right.

Daniel awoke with a start then smiled and pulled Megan's naked body closer to his. His eyes slid shut again with a contented sigh before they flew back open a second later. He reached for his phone and Megan stirred against him. When he saw that they'd only dozed off for about an hour, he reclaimed his spot and smoothed his hand over her back.

"Shhh. It's okay," he whispered. "You can sleep more."

She stretched languorously, her arched back pressing the front of her more firmly against him. His body responded instantly and his hand traveled down to cup and squeeze her round bottom. The depth of his desire for her made his stomach clench with nerves, but he couldn't stop aching for her even if he wanted to.

"Hmm." She smiled sleepily at him. "Are you sure you want me to go back to sleep? I'm getting mixed signals here."

He would never stop hungering for her, but more than anything, he wanted to wake up beside her in the morning. The thought startled him enough to bolt out of bed. He didn't do sleepovers. He didn't even bring women to his place as a rule. Whatever this was, he had to watch his step.

"I should take you home," he said, gathering his clothes off the floor.

She sat up slowly in bed with the cover held against

her chest. A hurt frown flitted across her face, but she said, "Okay."

"I don't want your father to worry," he mumbled, immediately contrite for his brusqueness.

"You're right." She dropped the sheet and got to her feet. Despite his sudden panic and need for space, he stared at her naked body like a man starved.

With her back turned to him, she slipped on her lingerie and stepped into her dress. She held up her hair in one hand and looked over her shoulder at him. "Do you mind?"

He wordlessly zipped up her gown while battling a wild need to rip it off her again. Because he needed to touch her, he rested his hands on her shoulders. After a pause, she turned around to face him, dislodging his hold.

"I can't have you drive me home," she said with a slight arch of her brow. "I don't want my father to know about our…fling. It would be cruel to give him false hope."

"Of course. I understand." He took a step back at her frostiness and stood taller to cover his inexplicable hurt. What had happened tonight was just sex. She didn't really want him. She'd walked out on him once before.

He tamped down on the bitterness churning inside him. He was being unreasonable. How else was she supposed to behave after he'd all but kicked her out of his bed? He followed her as she walked out to the living room to retrieve her clutch. Then he stood indecisively near the edge of the living room as she tapped into her phone.

"My ride should be here soon. I'll go wait down in the lobby." She glided toward the elevator, slipping on her shoes as she went.

"When will I see you again?" He caught her hand before she could press the down button. He had bungled this up, but he couldn't stand the thought of not seeing her again soon.

She twisted her hand out of his grasp and called the elevator. "The Chamber Music Society is hosting an event for its maestro's circle in a couple weeks. Walter Liu will be there."

"Megan," he said helplessly.

"I don't know what's going on with you right now, but you need to figure it out," she snapped. But her voice softened at something in his expression. "Daniel, this was just one night. Well…two nights. It doesn't have to happen again if you don't want it to."

"I want it to." His hands clenched and unclenched at his sides with the need to hold on to her. But he didn't want to *need to* hold on to her. He wanted simple and uncomplicated. It seemed as though that was exactly what Megan was offering him, but he was the one making it complicated. His chest felt taut with tension as though he was being ripped down the middle.

"I'm not sure I believe you," she said with quiet dignity. The elevator dinged and the doors slid open. With a fleeting kiss on his cheek, she stepped inside. "Good night."

The doors closed and he stood staring at his reflection on the polished metal. At least she hadn't said goodbye. That would have felt too permanent. Whatever happened, he would still see her at social events to carry out their plan and for her prenatal appointments. But he knew that wasn't enough anymore.

He thought he'd held himself back from wanting her—from having her—out of respect for Mr. Han and out of concern for Megan…but maybe it had been about himself all along. Maybe he'd been afraid of wanting more of Megan than he could have.

His father had always told him that women couldn't be trusted. Daniel had thought he was a bitter, old fool until…Sienna. She was so beautiful and vibrant. It felt as though he could warm up his cold, lonely existence just by being in her orbit. He couldn't believe his luck when the most sought-after girl in college wanted to date him. She could have anyone.

Daniel understood that only too well and he swore to do whatever he could to give her everything she wanted. But what she'd wanted was his roommate— the son of a wealthy senator. She had just used Daniel to get closer to him. When he confronted her after he found them in bed, she turned on him as though he was the one who had betrayed her.

Don't you want me to be happy for once? Sienna had said.

I could make you happy, he entreated.

I could never be happy with someone like you, she spat.

Women couldn't be trusted. His father had been right. His mother didn't think Daniel was worth sticking around for. Why would Sienna think otherwise? Why would Megan be any different?

He'd kept himself safe since Sienna. He had women in his life after her, but never allowed himself to become emotionally attached. As long as he didn't open himself up, he wouldn't get hurt when they left. It was better for everyone involved. The only thing he ever let himself want was to succeed. And he was almost there. He was the CFO of a major corporation. If he worked hard enough, he might someday become Jigu Corporation's CEO.

But when he had Megan in his arms, he was willing to risk everything he'd worked for to have her. She was still worth the risk—even more so with the smell of her lingering on his skin. But there was no reason to gamble his heart. He was wiser than that. He would only take what she gave him and wouldn't ask for anything more—wouldn't want anything more. They could have the now. *No promises*.

"Fuck," he breathed.

He shouldn't have let Megan leave like that. He'd made her think he regretted sleeping with her, when it was one of the most amazing nights of his life. He jabbed at the elevator button and hurried to retrieve his phone and keys. He ran back when he heard the ping of its arrival and slid between the doors before they closed on him.

Daniel rushed through the lobby and caught sight of her getting into her rideshare. He cursed under his breath and made a mad dash for the parking lot. If he broke some speed limits, he might be able to get to her house before she did.

When he'd arrived at the Han residence, the house was dark except for the exterior lights. He'd parked a few yards away and now stood in the shadows waiting for Megan. It was past midnight, but he didn't want to risk being seen by Mr. Han.

Now that he was here, he didn't know what to do. Had he beat her here? Or had she already gone inside? Would he sound like a lunatic if he called her and asked her to come outside? Just as he pulled his phone out of his back pocket, headlights shone into his eyes. He shielded them with his hand and squinted against the brightness. It was the car that Megan had gotten into.

He stepped toward it as it lurched to a halt—as though Megan had shouted for the driver to stop. She climbed out and walked up to him, looking magnificent in her red formal gown. She tugged him farther down the street, behind the shadow of a tall tree.

"What are you doing here?" Her voice was sharp with surprise.

"I acted like an idiot." He pulled her into his arms and held her close. "I don't regret what happened tonight. I… I have some baggage to deal with, but it's my problem, not yours."

"Daniel—" She held herself stiff against him.

"I want you, Megan," he said before she could continue. "Tell me I haven't blown this."

"I want you, too."

"Don't say *but*."

"But," she said, ignoring his request, "I don't want to push you into something you're not comfortable with…"

He couldn't lie to her. He wasn't at ease with the situation. Not with the secret pregnancy and not with adding a secret affair on top of it. Most of all, he was terrified at how much he wanted her. But none of that mattered if it meant he could have her—just for a little while.

"I don't think either of us are comfortable with lying to your father," he admitted to the half truth, dropping his arms down to his sides. "That's why we have to win over the board members, so we can tell your father that the baby is mine."

"And this?" She flapped her hand between them. "What do we tell him about this?"

"We'll figure that out when the time comes," he hedged.

"I see." A shuttered expression settled on her face. "You're right. Who knows? Maybe there won't be anything to tell him by then."

His stomach lurched with something like dread. He didn't want to think about when he would have to let her go—when she would leave him. He wanted to focus on keeping her by his side for now.

"We'll do this your way." He reached out to cup her face. "Take it day by day. No promises."

"Day by day." She took a deep breath and leaned into his touch. "No promises."

He placed a lingering kiss on her sweet, parted lips. She sighed and pressed herself against him. This was enough. He didn't need more than this. As long as he didn't get greedy, he would be able to let her go without bitterness or resentment. His love for the baby wouldn't be tainted by heartbreak. Everything was going to be just fine.

Eight

"How are you feeling?" Angie whispered to Megan as they took their seats in front of the small audience.

"Barely any jitters," Megan said with a shrug. "The maestro's circle is basically our fan club. They'll love everything we play for them."

"I wasn't asking about that." Her older sister sighed, then stared pointedly at her stomach.

"Ohhh." Megan laughed softly and caught herself before she placed her hand on her baby bump. "We're doing swell."

"Good." Angie's affectionate smile made Megan blink. She looked so much like their mom. "Glad to hear Nephew and Sister are both doing swell."

"Thank you, Unni." Megan turned to include Chloe. "All right, ladies. Are we ready?"

At her sisters' nods, she brought the violin under her chin and raised the bow. They all inhaled together, held their breath for a second, then Megan dropped her bow to the strings. She and her sisters exhaled as the music carried them away.

Schubert's *String Trio D 471* was both playful and deeply moving—simply beautiful in its complexity. The Hana Trio weaved through the depths and peaks of the piece with courage and vulnerability, the three of them supporting each other and lifting each other up. The trust between Megan and her sisters brought an added layer to the piece that was entirely their own.

As the last note and its vibrations faded, they lowered their bows. There was a moment of awed silence before applause erupted from the audience. Megan smiled at her sisters and the three of them stood and took their bow. The applause didn't die down until another group of their fellow musicians filed onto the stage.

The mezzanine of the concert hall was bustling with the most generous and well-dressed of the Chamber Music Society's donors when the performers joined the party. The royal blue-and-gold carpeting, dark wood trimming and crystal chandeliers gave the event the opulence and elegance befitting their guests of honor, the maestro's circle.

Daniel, while not a member of the maestro's circle yet, scored himself an invite, thanks to Angie. The Chamber Music Society owed Angie and Joshua for their part in revitalizing their organization when it was in dire straits after the pandemic. But even as she craned her neck this way and that, Megan couldn't find the damn man—which only meant one thing. He wasn't there. There was no way she could miss him, even in a crowd.

Then she saw him walking up the staircase with his tie slightly askew. His head swiveled left and right, and he raked his fingers through his hair, obviously not for the first time tonight. Megan was peeved he was late, but decided to give him a break and wove through the crowd toward him.

The frown on his face cleared when his eyes landed on her. "Megan."

"This is the second time you missed our performance," she said, crossing her arms over her chest. "I'm beginning to think that you would do anything to get out of listening to classical music."

"I'm sorry," he murmured. When she continued to glare at him, he moved closer and whispered, "I'm sorry, baby. Forgive me."

She couldn't hold back a shiver at the intimacy of his voice, which made her more cross. "You better have a good reason."

"Charity Hansen wanted to discuss something," he said.

"The board member Charity Hansen?"

"Yes, I thought it would be an excellent opportunity to get to know each other."

"Good thinking." Megan nodded. "We could use her on our side."

"I was hoping you'd say that." The last traces of worry left Daniel's face as he grinned down at her.

"But I'm really sorry I missed your performance. Perhaps…you could give me a private one later?"

Her heart fluttered and a blush rose to her cheeks.
"Perhaps."

His grin grew broader and decidedly naughtier,
but before he could continue, the rest of the Han sisters joined the conversation. Megan's stomach knot-
ted. They knew Daniel was the baby's father, but she
hadn't told them about their affair. She didn't want
to give them another secret to keep from their father.

"Shouldn't you be over there talking to Walter?"
Angie said pointedly to Daniel.

"Nice to meet you. You must be Angie," he said
with a smile. At least one of them remembered their
manners. "And nice to meet you, Chloe."

"Hi, Daniel." Chloe dimpled prettily at him. "But
you should really get over there and charm the hell
out of Mr. Liu. Keeping secrets from our dad makes
my stomach hurt."

"I'm sorry, Chloe," Megan said miserably.

"Me, too," Daniel said.

"We don't need apologies." Angie jerked her head
toward their target. "Go and work your magic, Megan.
And Daniel, try not to get in her way. But it was nice
meeting you as well."

"Okay." Megan placed her hand on Daniel's arm.
"We're going in."

Walter Liu and his wife had broken off from the
small group they were chatting with and stood alone,
speaking quietly to each other. But when they spotted Megan and Daniel approaching, Walter held his

arms wide. "Megan, my dear. You and your sisters were spectacular."

"Thank you, Mr. Liu." Megan hugged him and stepped back. "How are you, Mrs. Liu?"

"Getting old, but that's not something to complain about. It's a blessing." Annette Liu was small in stature but mighty in spirit. "And you are?"

"Hello, Mrs. Liu. I'm Daniel Pak," he said with a polite smile. "It's nice to meet you. And good to see you again, Mr. Liu."

Walter grunted in reply. Daniel was going to have to do better than that. Megan had to coax the charm out of him. "Since my father is out of town, the society invited Daniel as Jigu Corporation's representative. And he conveniently showed up right *after* the performances ended."

The tips of Daniel's ears turned a little pink and he widened his eyes at her. "For which I've profusely apologized."

Walter chuckled. "Megan, stop putting the man on the spot."

"Yes, Megan." Daniel cast a grateful glance at Mr. Liu. "Listen to his wise counsel."

"Don't worry, Mr. Liu," Megan said playfully. "Daniel and I are friends. I won't torment him too much."

"I think I should just stick with Mr. and Mrs. Liu for the rest of the evening," Daniel said, inching closer to them.

Megan couldn't hold back her laugh. Who could resist him when he was so endearing? Walter and Annett exchanged a knowing glance. *Here we go again.* Once her friends saw that Daniel was a decent guy, they immediately thought about matching him up with Megan. She was going to interpret that as a good sign that they would gladly take Daniel into their fold.

Soon. They would be able to tell her dad the truth soon. But not the whole truth, right? Her stomach swooped with anxiety. What could they tell him about what was happening between them? *We don't want to get married even though we made a baby together, but we really like having sex with no strings attached.* That would make any father proud. She cringed inwardly. But daughters didn't have to live their lives to please their fathers. They had to forge their own paths—follow their own instincts.

Despite her confidence in her instincts, Megan wondered if she had any *survival* instincts worth a damn. She knew with everything in her that Daniel Pak was a good man and she wanted him more than she'd ever wanted anyone else before. She could only assume that the teeny-tiny voice inside her, warning her that this wouldn't end well—that she would get her heart broken—was her survival instinct, but the little voice was much too easy to ignore. The drumming of her heart and the rush of blood in her head every time she was near him drowned it out.

The sound of laughter drew her out of her thoughts. With the ice broken, Daniel was winning the Lius with his brand of earnest charm. He always listened closely and responded with solemn honesty. She respected that. Sometimes being honest took courage because it also revealed a part of who you were... It made you vulnerable. She wondered if Daniel knew how brave he was to treat others with such deep respect.

"I'm having lunch with an old friend next week," Walter said. "I think you should join us, Daniel. He might have some wisdom to share with you about the industry. You're young, but you're a leader. You need to surround yourself with good people."

"Thank you so much, Mr. Liu," Daniel said.

"Call me Walter."

"Walter." Daniel smiled and handed him his business card. "This has my direct line. Please call me when you know the details and I'll be sure to join you."

"Good man." Mr. Liu pounded Daniel on the back.

"It was great seeing you, but we should go and make the rounds," Annette suggested, giving her husband a look. When he didn't budge, she tugged him away by his arms. "Give the young people some space, you old dolt."

"Bye, Mr. and Mrs. Liu," Megan said with a wave. She turned to Daniel with a smile. "Look at you. I don't think you even need my help anymore."

"Walter wouldn't have spared me a stiff smile if it hadn't been for you," he said, taking a step closer to her.

She pressed her index finger to his sternum and gently pushed. "Please maintain a friends-only distance. If you get too close, I might be tempted to kiss you."

His grin was blinding as he leaned into her touch

for a split-second before he stepped back. "How long do we have to stay?"

"Why?" She glanced at him from under her lashes. "Do you have someplace to be?"

"Yes." His eyes dropped to her lips and she could feel the heat emanating from him even from a respectable distance. "It's rather urgent."

"I have to smile and show my appreciation to all these generous donors." A shiver went down her spine at his frown of displeasure. "Give me thirty minutes and I'll meet you at your place."

"I'll give you twenty," he said with an arrogant arch of his eyebrow.

She would've laughed and teased him about how impatient he was if she wasn't busy holding herself back from jumping him in a room full of people. In the end, all she managed was a small whimper. With a knowing smile, Daniel walked past her, letting the back of his hand lightly graze hers.

She glanced down expecting to see a tendril of smoke wafting up from her hand. *You're in so much trouble*, her survival instinct squeaked.

"Oh, shut up," she muttered. "I have no time for your puny warnings."

Megan had to pull off the fastest smile-and-greet she'd ever done so she could go running into her lover's arms.

Daniel felt his mouth go dry as he watched Megan glide toward him across the lobby in her strapless black dress. Her bare shoulders and sophisticated updo accentuated the alluring line of her neck, and he became frenzied with the desire to nip and lick the sensitive skin there. He'd seen her in a formal dress before, but the simple elegance she exuded tonight made him desperate to *undo* her.

When she came to stand in front of him, he forced himself to glance down at his watch and drawl, "You're late. I said twenty minutes."

Her lashes fluttered and her lips parted. God, she wanted him as much as he wanted her.

"I'm not late," she said in a husky voice. "Your watch is fast."

"Excuses, excuses." He reached behind him and called the elevator to his penthouse.

"I don't need to make excuses." She raised her chin in challenge, but anticipation glinted in her eyes. "You don't get to tell me what to do."

"Is that so?" he crooned softly, even though he felt light-headed with arousal.

He guided her inside the elevator and pushed her up against the back wall as soon as the doors closed behind them.

"You kept me waiting," he said into her ear with his hands planted by her head, imprisoning her with his arms and body. "You're going to make it up to me."

"H-how?" She bit her bottom lip as she waited for her instructions.

"Unzip your dress," he said, leaning back just enough to allow her to reach behind her. Her eyes didn't leave his as she lowered her zipper. "Good girl."

He grabbed the front of her bodice and roughly

tugged it down so she was naked from the waist up. Megan's sharp gasp shot straight to his groin. He'd forgotten that they were in an elevator until the doors opened behind them. He wrapped his hands around her waist and spun them around, and marched her backward out of the elevator.

"Take the rest of your clothes off." He stepped back from her and crossed his arms over his chest.

She shimmied the dress past her hips and down to her ankles, and kicked it away from her. She stood proud, clad only in her panties and high heels. Her breasts were fuller than the first night they'd been together and her softly rounded stomach drew his eyes. He was gripped by a dizzying need to possess her.

"Touch me," she said with a hint of impatience.

"Go stand behind the sofa." When she opened her mouth to protest, he cut her off with a command. "Now."

Her cheeks flushed red and her chest rose and fell with every quickening breath. She slowly spun on her heels and made her way to the sofa. The sway of her hips hypnotized him and he stood rooted to the spot until she glanced over her shoulder with a sultry smile. He caught up with her just as she stopped at the sofa and turned to face him.

"Turn around," he said in a gravelly voice he hardly recognized as his own, "and bend over."

A shuddering breath escaped past her lips and she did as she was told. He almost lost it in his pants when she bent over the back of the sofa, thrusting her sweet, round ass toward him. He gripped one side of her waist, his fingers digging into her flesh, and un-buckled his belt with the other hand. Megan whim-pered and restlessly bucked her hips.

He drew himself out and dragged his tip through her slick folds before placing himself at her entrance. "Do you want this?"

"Yes," she moaned.

"Yes, what?" He was shaking with his need for her, and sweat slid down his temples.

"Yes, I want you," she said breathlessly. "I want you inside of me. Please."

Daniel thrust inside her and groaned, his head fall-ing back. God, she felt so good. Suddenly, he came to his senses. She was soft, wet and ready for him, but had he been too rough?

"Megan." He smoothed his hands over her waist. "Are you okay, baby?"

In response, she swiveled her hips. "Daniel, please."

He needed no further encouragement. He felt like his mind was splintering with the need to have her, and he said her name again and again as he pounded into her. He was losing control. He couldn't hold on much longer.

"Baby, I need you to come." His fingers found her nub, and he pressed and rubbed her in rhythm with their coupling. "Come for me."

With a low cry, her muscles clenched around him and he joined her in the climax. Waves of pleasure pulsed through him with a force that nearly made his knees buckle. He came back to the present when he felt Megan shivering beneath his hands. He didn't want to leave her warmth yet, but he pulled himself out and lifted her into his arms. He carried her to his bed and collapsed beside her.

As he pulled the covers over her naked body, he realized that he was still fully dressed. He hadn't even taken his blazer off. Shaking his head in wonder, he got up from the bed to undress and joined her again under the covers. He needed to be close to her.

He put his hand on her shoulder and smoothed it down her arm. She had stopped shivering, but she hadn't said a word. Uneasiness shot through him. What had gotten into him? He seemed to lose his mind around her.

"Megan…"

She shifted to her side so she was facing him. Slowly, a wide smile spread across her face and laughter bubbled out of her. "That was fucking amazing."

"I don't know what happened," he murmured almost to himself. "I've never wanted anyone before as much as I've wanted you."

He stiffened as soon as the words left his mouth, but Megan cupped his face and simply said, "Me, too."

A breath he didn't know he was holding left him in a rush and he crushed his lips against hers. He only drew back when his lungs demanded air. She stared at him with wide eyes, her swollen lips parted. Tenderness rushed through him and he ran his index finger down the bridge of her nose, then kissed the tip.

"Are you sure you're okay?" he asked.

"I'll probably be a little sore." She stretched languidly beside him and lay with her back to him. "But it was totally worth it."

"Good," he said, spooning her snuggly from behind. "By the way, do you really think I don't like classical music?"

"I was just teasing...but *do* you like classical music?" She wrapped his arm firmly around her midriff.

"I love classical music." He nibbled her shoulder. "I even hear it when I make love to you."

"What?" She giggled. "Which piece?"

"Handel's *Messiah*." He grinned against her skin. *"Hallelujah. Hallelujah, hallelujah..."*

"You're such an idiot," she said with a smile in her voice. "But I guess you do love classical music."

He'd always appreciated classical music, but knowing that Megan was a part of that world made the music almost seem like magic now. Having classical music playing in the background throughout his day made him feel close to her. It stopped him from missing her so much that he would drop everything to run to her.

Daniel didn't look too closely at why he wanted to feel close to her. It was desire like he'd never known before. It consumed him. And they had a connection. She made him feel comfortable in his own skin.

When their passion was spent, he hoped they could be friends. Friendship didn't come with any messy emotional entanglement. And even if it ended, friendship would never wreck him enough to tarnish his love for his child. Yes, friendship would be his end goal for this relationship. That would make coparenting that much easier and more enjoyable.

He drifted off to sleep and dreamed of sunny days, picnicking in the park. He was too far gone to think it odd that he carried their son in one arm and had the other wrapped around Megan with his hand resting on her round, pregnant belly. It didn't seem odd at all that they were growing their family. After all, he didn't want his son to be an only child like him. In the dream, he knew he would do anything to keep his family together…even offer Megan his heart. His dream-self threw his head back and laughed at the absurdity of his thought. His heart was already hers.

Nine

Considering how thin Megan was from her morning sickness, it was hard to mistake her baby bump for anything other than what it was, especially in her stretchy maternity pants and fitted shirt with Peter Pan collars. The whispers started the moment she walked onto the stage to join the Chamber Orchestra for rehearsal. She'd been asked to fill in for the second violin, who was away on a family emergency. The conductor hadn't joined them yet, so there was time for her fellow musicians to process their surprise.

"Congratulations, my dear." The principal flutist was the first to approach. She surreptitiously checked her ring finger to make sure Megan hadn't gotten married overnight. "Most of us have an artist's heart, so there's no need to fret about censure. But if you do want me to circulate an official story of sorts, I'll be happy to spread the word to temper the gossip."

"Thank you, Tiffany." Megan smiled warmly at the older woman. She was a talented musician and a professional through and through, but she also had a kind heart. "I'd like that. It would take some heat off my sisters as well."

"Of course." Tiffany looked askance at her when she didn't speak right away.

"Oh, right." Megan shook her head. "The official story. The pregnancy came as a surprise but the baby's father and I are looking forward to parenthood."

The flutist raised her eyebrows at the very brief explanation but nodded and returned to her seat. Megan shared enough to prevent anyone from painting her as the poor little pregnant woman abandoned by her callous lover. Without that bit of drama, the gossip wouldn't be juicy enough to last long.

Megan didn't linger after the rehearsal and headed straight to her car—not to avoid people, but because she had a date with Daniel in a couple of hours. Her heart picked up pace and made a ruckus in her chest. It couldn't be because she got to see Daniel—she'd seen him last night for God's sake—but because she got to see one of her favorite musicians play tonight.

Child prodigy turned virtuoso, violinist Anthony Larsen was only eight years her senior, but she'd watched him perform since she was a little girl. The violin pieces she knew and loved became something new and dynamic with Anthony's energetic and passionate interpretations. As the years passed, his performances only became richer and more nuanced without losing an ounce of passion. She didn't think she'd ever shared her awe of the violinist with Daniel, but to her delight, he had secured them two orchestra seats to Anthony Larsen's concert.

Once she got home, Megan took her time with her bath and styled her hair with loose curls. She applied her makeup with a light touch, using a petal-pink lipstick for both her cheeks and lips. Just as she pushed back from her vanity, she heard a knock at her bedroom door.

"Megan?" It was Mrs. Chung.

"Come in," she said, turning around to face the door.

"I brought you some sandwiches." Their housekeeper strode into her room with a tray laden with enough finger sandwiches for five people. She had been feeding Megan every two hours since she found out about the pregnancy. "You must be hungry."

"You don't give me a chance to get hungry." Megan laughed. "But maybe I am a little peckish…"

A huge smile spread across Mrs. Chung's face as she set out the sandwiches and lemonade on the coffee table in the sitting area. "The little darling is busy growing."

"Yes, he must be. Thank you, Mrs. Chung."

After eating a plate full of dainty sandwiches, Megan walked into her closet and fingered through her dresses suited for an evening at a concert. She opted for a simple boatneck dress in black with enough stretch to accommodate her growing stomach. She added a gold pendant necklace to her ensemble and reapplied the lipstick she'd eaten off with her snack.

Her father wouldn't be home for a few hours, but she had insisted on meeting Daniel at the concert venue. She didn't want to tempt fate by having him pick her up here. They only had a couple more board members to woo, then they could tell her father the truth about the baby's father. She still had no idea how to explain her relationship with Daniel—or if she would tell her father anything about it at all. If it was just a temporary fling, there was no use upsetting him any more than they had to.

But Megan knew that it was not a casual fling for her. It had never been. The question was... Was she going to do anything about it? She'd told him she didn't need promises and she'd meant it. She had wanted him even if it was only for a fleeting moment. She couldn't stop herself from hoping for more, though.

Daniel wanted her. She knew that. But what kept him from opening up to her? Why couldn't something real bloom between them? With a sickening lurch of her stomach, she wondered if he was in love with someone else. Someone back East? An old flame? Maybe someone unattainable. She sighed. Letting her imagination run wild wasn't going to help anyone, especially her.

The drive to the concert felt like an eternity. She needed to see Daniel. When they were together, it felt as though she belonged to him. They were discreet about their relationship, but he couldn't hide the slight quirk of his lips whenever their eyes met, and he couldn't seem to stop himself from touching her—innocuous and light—every chance he got.

Daniel had given Megan her ticket in case he was detained at work, so she went inside and took a seat. She willed her legs not to bounce as she waited for him, but she found herself tapping her index finger on the armrest. She curled her fingers and held tight to the armrest to stop herself from fidgeting.

"Hi." Daniel slid into the seat next to her and offered her a crooked smile. His smiles came much more easily now, and she couldn't help but feel a little responsible for that. "See? I can be on time for classical music."

Her breath left her in a shaky sigh, but she said, "I guess it's only when I'm the one performing that you run late."

"I'm still waiting for that private performance." He chuckled and brushed his knee against hers.

She shivered at the barely there touch, but its familiarity comforted her. The lights dimmed before she could respond, and they turned their attention to the stage. Anthony's music seemed to suck the oxygen out of the concert hall, and Megan watched and listened, holding her breath. But everything in her relaxed as he played Brahms's *Hungarian Dance No. 1*. The beauty of the song brought tears to her eyes and she reached for Daniel's hand in the darkness. His fingers tangled with hers, but his enthralled gaze remained on the violinist.

The music brought her emotions close to the surface and she stared in awe at the beautiful man sitting beside her. No, a short fling was not what she wanted. She wanted Daniel to be hers—heart, body and soul. Was she willing to act on her desire?

Megan couldn't stop to consider whether *her* heart already belonged to him. Then she would be too afraid to act. She wanted him. All of him. She would leave it at that for now. And she wouldn't *say* anything to Daniel. There couldn't be promises without words, right? She would show him that she wanted him by her side with her actions.

Anthony Larsen dove into his rendition of Bizet's "Habanera" from *Carmen*, which brought entirely different emotions to the surface. Megan squirmed in her seat, much too aware of the heat coming off Daniel's body. He ran his thumb over the sensitive skin on her palm. When she turned to glance at him, his gaze focused on her, and everyone else in the room melted away. Her chest rose and fell with each quickening breath as the heat in his eyes slowly burned through her body.

The resounding applause brought her out of the trance, and she rose from her seat and joined the rest of the audience in a standing ovation. Anthony bowed and walked off the stage for intermission and the applause finally quieted.

"Come on." Daniel's hand settled on the small of her back. "I want you to meet someone."

She only had time to quirk her eyebrow as he propelled her through the crowd toward the front of the auditorium. She finally spoke up when he gave his name to a security guard, who opened the door to the backstage area. "Where are we going?"

"Daniel." Anthony Larsen walked up to them and pulled Daniel into a one-armed hug. "It's good to see you, man."

"Good to see you, too." Daniel returned the bro hug before stepping back. "Anthony, this is my...friend, Megan Han."

Something clenched painfully in her chest at the term. She was being ridiculous. Hadn't she introduced him the same way to all the board members? But that had been different. They were her father's friends and they'd agreed to keep their relationship a secret from him. Anthony, it seemed, was Daniel's friend. She shook off her pointless sense of hurt when the violinist beamed at her.

"Megan, it is an absolute pleasure to meet you," he said, pumping her hand enthusiastically. His light brown hair fell into his striking hazel eyes, making him look boyish and charming. "You and your sisters are incredible musicians. I'm a true fan. I can't believe we haven't run into each other before now."

Her mouth opened and closed several times before she could form proper words. "I've hero-worshipped you since I was four. The pleasure is all mine."

"Okay. Now you've gone and made me feel old." Anthony chuckled a bit sheepishly.

She realized he was embarrassed by her fangirling

and decided that she liked him—not the musician but the man—immediately. She was glad he wasn't the superficial playboy the gossip columns painted him to be. Not that she gave them much credence in the first place.

"Hardly," she said with an easy smile. "You were all of twelve yourself."

"We should let you rest and prepare for the second half," Daniel said. "I knew you were going to be bombarded with reporters and fans after the show, so I wanted to come by to say hello and introduce you to Megan."

"I appreciate that." Anthony's gaze turned a bit speculative as it rested on her before he turned back to Daniel. "But you and I should meet up later tonight. I have something for you."

"Yes, right." Daniel nodded quickly. "I'll come by your hotel. Around eleven?"

"That works. See you then." Her idol turned to her with a brilliant smile. "Glad to finally meet you. Will you introduce me to your sisters next time I'm in town?"

"Oh, they wouldn't let me hear the end of it if I didn't," Megan said honestly. Chloe used to have a huge crush on Anthony Larsen in her tender teenage years.

When they left the backstage, Daniel asked, "Would you like something to drink? We still have a few more minutes until intermission ends."

"No, thanks. I have to pee." Megan crinkled her nose. "I always have to pee these days."

"That must be a hassle." Something tender flitted across Daniel's face as if she'd said something endearing. "I'll wait for you here, then."

"Don't be silly." She felt herself blushing for some reason. "I can find my way back to my seat. Go get settled. I'll be right there."

The line at the restroom was longer than she'd expected and the lights were blinking to signal the end of intermission by the time she arrived at her seat.

"I thought you got lost," Daniel teased, leaning close to her ear as the lights dimmed.

She only had time to stick her tongue out at him before the concert resumed. The only things she was aware of were the music and the warmth of Daniel's hand in hers. When she turned to look at him yet again, he met her eyes in the semi-darkness, as though he felt her gaze on him. She smiled at him with her heart and the corners of his lips turned up in response.

No, she didn't need words to tell him that she wanted him by her side. She would tell him with her whole being.

"Scotch?" Anthony asked him.

"Oh, yeah." Daniel settled back into the plush couch of his friend's hotel suite and accepted the glass of amber liquid. "Thanks."

He'd had a hard time parting with Megan after the concert. Something had shifted between them tonight. He could feel it. He could feel *her*. Her warmth and affection infused him with emotions he couldn't begin to identify—emotions he didn't want to identify. He wasn't sure what he was more afraid of...his own feelings? Or of losing that sense of *rightness* with Megan?

"All right." Nursing his own drink, Anthony plopped down on the sofa next to him. "I'm ready. Spill it."

"Spill what?" He took a sip of his Scotch, enjoying its smooth heat as it went down his throat.

His friend scoffed and aimed straight for the jugular. "Who is she?"

Daniel stopped pretending he didn't know what Anthony was talking about. "She's a...friend."

"You bought a Stradivarius for a *friend*?" Anthony's eyebrows rose high on his forehead.

"She's a friend who is...pregnant with my child," Daniel said quietly. "We're coparenting partners."

"Holy shit. A baby?" His friend took a big gulp of Scotch. "And that's all she is to you?"

"Isn't that enough?" Daniel glanced down at his drink. It had to be enough.

"I saw the way you looked at her." Anthony leveled him with a no-bullshit stare. "She's more than a friend or a coparenting partner to you."

"Think what you want," he said with a shrug.

"She couldn't be the musician that she is if she wasn't strong, dedicated and courageous." Anthony paused for a beat. "She is nothing like Sienna."

"I know that," Daniel scoffed as though he truly believed it. But he knew Megan would leave him just as his mother and Sienna had done. Why would someone like her stick around for him?

"You can't let one bad relationship dictate your life," Anthony pushed.

"Oh, that's rich," Daniel drawled. "We both know you're in no position to give relationship advice."

He immediately regretted lashing out at his friend when Anthony's face paled. He was a dick.

"Shit." Daniel tugged his hand through his hair. "Anthony…"

"You're absolutely right. What would a *player* know about relationships?" Anthony said with a smile that held a tinge of sadness. "Let's not waste time talking about women. We have a lot to catch up on."

Daniel hadn't been able to get Megan out of his mind—the soft brush of her hand against his on the arm of the chair…the warmth of her gaze in the dim concert hall. He'd hardly slept, desperate to have her in his arms. And he asked himself for the umpteenth time what the Stradivarius violin in his closet meant. Damn Anthony and his prying questions.

"Wouldn't you agree?" Walter Liu said, wiping his mouth with a cloth napkin. He'd invited Daniel to lunch as promised.

"I'm sure I do—" it took Daniel two full seconds to realize he'd been asked a question "—but you're going to have to repeat everything you said before that, because my mind wandered for a minute."

Chris Tanner, another longtime member of Jigu Corporation's board of directors, roared with a belly laugh. "Your story clearly bored the man silly, Walter."

"Not at all," Daniel said sheepishly. "I'm running

on less than four hours of sleep. It's making me day-
dream about my bed."

Everything he said was true except that his day-
dreams about his bed usually included Megan. He
took a long sip of ice water to cool down his thoughts
and wake himself up. He and Anthony hadn't seen
each other in close to a year, so catching up—and
emptying a bottle of Scotch—had taken longer than
practical for a weeknight. Tossing and turning, dream-
ing of Megan all night, probably hadn't helped either.

"Or you might be being diplomatic by not par-
ticipating in our roasting of the venerable Minsung
Han," Walter Liu said with a good-natured chuckle.
The mention of Megan's father made Daniel's stomach
twist uncomfortably. Guilt was a bitch. "But a word of
advice…you're young but you're not invincible. You
need food and sleep like any other human being."

"Well, being Minsung's protégé, he's bound to be a
workaholic like him," Chris added, pointing his fork
at Daniel. "Even so, I agree with Walter about the ne-
cessity of food and sleep."

"Speaking of food, thank you for letting me join
you for lunch." Daniel took a bite out of his club sand-
wich, hoping it would settle his churning stomach.

This lunch brought him one step closer to telling
Mr. Han that he was the baby's father. But would it
be the whole truth? He knew, but didn't want to acknowledge, that the only way to truly assuage his guilt
would be to stop sleeping with the CEO's daughter behind his back. Even the thought of letting Megan go,
however, made his blood run cold. He would rather

live with the guilt, even if that made him an ungrateful bastard.

He managed to focus on the conversation for the rest of lunch, which he enjoyed more than he'd expected. Walter and Chris were wise, intelligent and very much not full of themselves. He had a lot to learn from them. They parted with a promise to get together again soon.

Daniel had left himself plenty of time to make it to Megan's prenatal appointment, so he was sitting on the bench outside the medical building, checking his email, when she walked up to him.

"You don't have to come to every one of my appointments, you know," she said by way of greeting. "This one won't be very exciting. There isn't even going to be an ultrasound or anything."

"It doesn't matter." He got to his feet, pocketing his phone. "I want to hear for myself that you and the baby are doing well."

"What? My word isn't good enough?" she asked, arching her eyebrow.

"You're not a medical doctor, are you?" He took a gentle hold of her elbow and led them inside the building.

Once she'd checked in, Megan handed him her purse and said, "I have to go pee in a cup. Wait for me here."

"I wasn't planning on going anywhere," he said with wry grin.

She walked off with a huff. She seemed cranky

today. It was kind of cute, but he hoped nothing was wrong.

They didn't have to wait long to be shown to an examination room, and the doctor joined them soon with a cheerful knock on the door.

"Hello," Dr. Pinkus said. "Good to see you guys. So how are you feeling today?"

"I feel good…" Megan chewed her bottom lip. "But I haven't felt the baby move, yet. Is…is that normal?"

Daniel shot her a sharp glance. She sounded nervous. If she'd been so worried, why hadn't she said anything to him? He held his breath as he waited for the doctor's answer.

"Let's see." The doctor flipped through her chart. "You're at twenty-two weeks, right?"

"Yes," Megan said in a near whisper.

"It's perfectly normal not to feel the baby move yet, especially for a first pregnancy." Dr. Pinkus smiled reassuringly. "There's absolutely no reason to worry. It'll happen sometime in the second trimester. You still have a ways to go."

"Okay." Megan's shoulders slumped with relief. "Thank you, Doctor."

The doctor ran through a series of routine questions and nodded with satisfaction. "You're doing great, my dear."

Daniel finally felt himself relax, but his heart still pounded uncomfortably in his chest. He didn't speak until they stepped into the afternoon sun.

"Why didn't you tell me? If you were worried about

not feeling the baby move, why didn't you say anything?"

"You're not a medical doctor, are you?" She mimicked his words, but her eyes were soft with understanding. "I didn't tell you because I knew you would react like this. This way, you were only freaked out for a couple of minutes."

"Next time, you don't need to spare me the worry." He stopped in front of her car and placed his hands on her shoulders. "I told you I wanted to be here for you. Let me shoulder the concerns with you. You don't need to do this alone."

Her breath left her in a tremulous rush. "Goddammit, Daniel."

His eyebrows rose on his forehead. He didn't know what response he'd expected, but that wasn't it. Neither did he expect her to tug his head down and kiss him senseless in the middle of the parking lot.

When she leaned back and glowered at him, he said, "I'm not sure I understand what's going on here, but could we continue this at my place?"

Her lips quirked up at the corners, but she quickly pulled them down. "Don't you have to get back to work?"

"I'll be useless at the office after that kiss," he said in a low growl.

This time she didn't hold back her smile. "Well, in that case…"

His cell phone started ringing just as their lips were about to meet again. He planned on ignoring it, but Megan put a hand on his chest and pushed him back.

"You'd better get that."

"Shit," he muttered when he saw that it was his executive assistant. "Yes, Terri."

She wanted to know if he could move up his dinner meeting to an hour from now. The investment banker he was scheduled to meet had to fly out of the country for an urgent business matter later in the evening and wouldn't be back in town for at least a week.

"Have him come into the office. I'll be back—" he glanced at his watch "—in forty-five minutes."

Daniel stuffed his phone back in his jacket and sighed. "Megan…"

"I know," she said with a shrug. "Duty calls. You shouldn't have tried to play hooky in the first place."

He grabbed her by the shoulders and kissed her firmly on the lips. "Have dinner with me tonight?"

"Okay. Sure. Dinner sounds good." She sounded a little breathless, and her eyes were glued to his lips.

He couldn't stop the wolfish grin that spread across his face. "After dinner, we'll finish what we started."

"Twice." Her gaze finally rose to meet his and the seductive promise in them sucked the breath out of him.

The power she held over him sang in his blood, and a part of him desperately wanted to answer the siren's call. But a bigger part of him told him to run and hide—to keep himself safe.

He would do neither. He wouldn't let her go—he couldn't—but he wouldn't fall for her. He had to protect himself and remember that he wasn't meant to be loved. She would leave him eventually. That was inevitable. He just had to make sure that she didn't take his heart with her.

Ten

Megan tapped her foot as the elevator climbed to the penthouse. Daniel's afternoon meeting had run long, so their dinner got pushed back. Time had already been crawling at a snail's pace ever since they parted at the parking lot of her ob-gyn's office. Needless to say, she was impatient to see him. She couldn't decide whether to throw herself at him the moment the elevator doors opened or to kick him in the shin for keeping her waiting. She must be very hungry for those to be the only two options she could think of.

But she ended up doing neither when she reached the penthouse, because the smell of meat and butter assailed her nostrils. Plus, Daniel wasn't waiting for her in front of the elevator like he usually did. She followed her nose straight to the kitchen.

He was standing over the stove, barefoot in a plain white T-shirt and snug jeans. She wasn't sure what was making her mouth water more—the smell of the delicious food or the sight of the gorgeous man in front of her.

"You're cooking?" she managed to get out past her suddenly tight throat.

"It's only steak." He looked up from the pan with a distracted smile. "There's sparkling water in the fridge, if you're thirsty."

"*Only* steak?" She grabbed a bottle from the fridge and poured herself a tall glass. "You didn't even know where to look for tea in this kitchen."

"I still don't know where my housekeeper put the tea," he said, carefully basting the two steaks with what looked like melted butter infused with garlic and rosemary. "But just because I don't know where things are in *this* kitchen doesn't mean that I don't know my away around a kitchen."

"Where did you learn to cook?" She hopped onto a stool and took a long drink of her sparkling water.

"Home." Something in his voice made her frown, but she couldn't see his expression because he had his back turned to her. When she thought he wouldn't continue, he said, "I had to learn how to cook or live off of cold cereal."

Her frown deepened as she felt a painful tug in her heart. "You don't talk about your parents much."

"I never knew my mother." The very evenness of his tone told Megan of the pain hidden behind his words. "In a way, I guess I could say the same thing about my father. I lived at home with him until I went to college, but I might as well have lived alone."

She wanted to go to him, but the stiff way he held himself told her that he wouldn't welcome her sympathy. Her father had always been busy, but Megan had never doubted that he loved her. And she always had her mom and her sisters. It broke her heart that her sweet, kind Daniel had never known his parents' love—that he had to grow up so alone.

"Okay. It's ready," he said with determined cheerfulness. "I hope you're hungry."

"I'm starving." She forced her lips into a smile and helped him set the table. Once they were seated across from each other, she said, "What? No candles?"

His huff of laughter sounded genuine. "I don't think I have any. Even if I did, I wouldn't know where to find the matches."

"Well, I guess I'll let it pass this time since you did make me dinner." She eagerly sliced into her steak and stuffed a good-sized chunk into her mouth. Her eyes fluttered shut. "Mmm. I think I'd like to have this steak as my last meal."

"*I* think you're just really hungry," he said, but couldn't hide the pleasure from his voice.

Dinner was delicious, but Megan had to admit that her favorite part was the dessert. With a contented sigh, she snuggled against Daniel and tangled their legs under the sheets.

"Thank you for making me dinner." Then she thought it only polite to add, "and for the orgasms."

"Mmm-hmm." He sounded distracted and his fingers drummed against her shoulder blade where he was resting his hand.

"Hey." She glanced up at him. "Where's *my* thank-you?"

Finally, he laughed and kissed the tip of her nose. "Thank you for the orgasm. Thank you for the privilege of making you come. Thank you—" he leaned back and placed his hand on her stomach "—for carrying my child."

The heartfelt sincerity in his expression silenced the flippant response she had ready. "You're welcome."

"Wait here." He flung back the covers and slipped his jeans over his slim, bare hips.

She rose onto one elbow and watched him hurry to his closet. He reappeared carrying a violin case in his hand. Confusion drawing her eyebrows down, she sat up with the cover held over her breasts.

He carefully laid the violin case on the bed in front of her. His Adam's apple bobbed in his throat before he said, "Open it."

Megan reached out with one hand and unlatched the case. Her heart was pounding so hard she could feel it against the hand she held against her chest. Based on Daniel's expression, this wasn't an ordinary violin. She was almost afraid to see what was inside.

Her shocked gasp filled the room and the sheet she held against her fell to her lap as she reached for the violin with her trembling hands. "Daniel, what is this?"

"It—" he cleared his throat "—it's a Stradivarius."

"I know it's a Stradivarius," she said as she stared down at the violin, slowly turning it over this way and that. "What's it doing in your house? On your bed?"

"I want you to have it," he said simply.

"Why?" Her eyes finally rose to his face.

His expression held no hint of the nervousness he showed a moment ago. The hard line of his mouth and the grim set of his jaws masked his emotions. What was he afraid of revealing?

"I want you to have it," he repeated and shrugged with forced casualness. "You're having my baby and there's so little I could do to help. I just wanted to thank you properly."

Megan hadn't realized she was holding her breath until her chest started burning. She deliberately released it through her mouth. What had she been hoping he would say? That he had been an idiot for thinking that love and forever were a fairy tale that he could never give her? That this precious treasure was a token of his enduring love? Yes, that was what she had hoped he would say, because…she loved him. And she desperately wanted him to love her back.

"A Stradivarius is a bit excessive for a thank-you gift, don't you think?" She forced a lightness to her voice that she didn't feel. "Daniel, this couldn't have costed a penny less than two million dollars."

"It used to belong to Juliet Hannon," he said, watching her face closely.

"*The* Juliet Hannon? The legendary violinist? I thought she was taking a sabbatical." Megan cocked her head to the side. "Why would she sell her violin?"

"She's going to announce her retirement. She has Parkinson's, Megan."

"Oh, no." Her hand flew to her mouth and tears filled her eyes.

"She wanted her violin to go to someone who would love it and care for it just as she had." Daniel sat on the edge of the bed and placed his hand on her knee. "Ms. Hannon is Anthony's friend and mentor. When he shared the situation with me, I immediately thought of you. And they both agreed that you were a worthy successor for the Stradivarius. She sold me the violin at cost."

So many thoughts and feelings were tumbling through her, but she only managed to say, "But that must still be over a million dollars."

"It's not something I could return." He gave her a small smile.

"You should've discussed it with me," she said weakly, still holding on to the violin.

"I wanted it to be a gift from me." He ran his thumb across her wet cheek. She hadn't realized she was crying.

He cared about her. He cared about her enough to buy her a Stradivarius. It wasn't about the extravagance of the gift. He knew what it would mean to her. He knew she would strive to uphold the trust Juliet Hannon placed in her. He knew…her.

It wasn't enough. Megan deserved to be loved wholeheartedly. But it gave her hope—hope that if she fought for his love, she might actually win it.

"I can't accept this…" Something closed off in his

expression and she rushed to add, "But I also can't refuse something so precious."

"What are you saying?" He watched her warily.

"I don't have the willpower to stop myself from playing this violin, but you will be the only one to hear me play it. I want to keep this at your place." She put her finger on his lips when he began to protest. "For now. You have to let me think this through, Daniel."

He nodded, so she took her hand back. His face was still carefully neutral, but he looked more or less himself. She didn't know what was in her expression, but Daniel put his hand on the back of her neck and pulled her in for a hard, possessive kiss.

"I can't believe you gave me a Stradivarius while I'm naked," she said a little breathlessly when he released her. "It's a freaking Stradivarius. It deserves more respect."

He seemed to belatedly realize that other than a thin sheet loosely covering her legs, she was still completely nude. His eyes darkened as they took in her breasts. "You are magnificent naked. The Stradivarius should be honored."

She rolled her eyes even though she felt a blush spread across her chest and face. She gingerly placed the violin back in its case and got out of bed. Without bothering to put on her bra or underwear—the night was still young and Daniel was bound to undress her again—she pulled her oversize tunic over her head and declared herself presentable.

"Make yourself comfy," she said, reaching reverently for the violin.

She was both eager and nervous to try out the Stradivarius, and something about giving Daniel a private performance felt deeply intimate. Like she was baring her soul to him.

Blowing out a shaky breath, she brought the violin under her chin. "Let's see what this baby can do."

Megan had a performance face. It was an expression he'd never seen her make. It was one of intense concentration and immersion. There was a faint groove above the bridge of her nose and one eyebrow was delicately arched. That, of course, wasn't the first thing he noticed, but it was something he cached away in his mental file for everything Megan.

The first thing he noticed—no, felt, with every cell of his body—was the music. She'd chosen a piece lush with romance and passion. The soulful tune vibrated against his skin and bore into his heart. Listening to it while sitting on the edge of his bed, shirtless and barefoot, made him feel powerless against the beauty of the piece—powerless against the talented woman creating such music. By the time Megan opened her eyes and brought the violin and bow down to her sides, his hands were shaking so badly that he had them curled into tight fists on top of his thighs.

"That was just a snippet from a violin concerto…" she began uncertainly when he continued to sit silently.

"Wieniawski," he pushed past his dry throat. *"Violin Concerto No. 2 in D minor, Op. 22."*

"You know this piece." Surprise intermingled with

pleasure in her voice. "So you weren't bullshitting me when you said you enjoy classical music."

"No, I wasn't. I like listening to classical music, but I honestly don't know all that much about it. This concerto just happens to be a favorite of mine." He rubbed the back of his head. "I heard Anthony perform it a few years back and something about it touched me."

With a small smile, she lovingly placed the violin back in its case and closed it shut. "Well, if you've heard Anthony play it, then my performance might've been a letdown."

"You were incredible." He clasped his hand around her wrist and pulled her onto his lap. "I feel bewitched."

"Thank you," she said shyly. "For the compliment and for the Stradivarius. It responds like no other violin I've ever played, and the sound took my breath away."

"You're welcome." Relief rushed through him. A part of him had still been afraid that she would reject his gift. Her acceptance meant that she trusted him—that he was more than a casual fling to her. She wouldn't cast aside without a second thought.

"If you liked the private performance so much, you should come to one of my actual performances." She wrapped her arms around his neck. "I sound better in a concert hall. Your bedroom doesn't have very good acoustics."

"It was the best live performance I've ever heard." He smoothed his hand down her bare thighs. "And you played it only for me so I could claim it as mine."

"Hmm." She spread her legs and straddled his hips. He remembered with a burst of heat that she wore nothing under her tunic. "Do you want to claim my music? Or…me?"

She was just being playful. She couldn't know how desperately he wanted to claim her—to make her his. But he shied away from the thought. Claiming her meant giving himself to her as well, and he couldn't do that. He swore never to make himself vulnerable again—never to put himself in a position to be abandoned again.

"I want to claim your music." He lifted her shirt over her head, and she pressed her breasts against his chest. He wouldn't claim her heart, but her body could be his for tonight. He wouldn't let himself want more than that. They were taking this day by day. Tomorrow she might not be his, and he had to be okay with that. "I want to claim your body."

For a moment, her teasing smile turned sad and he felt his stomach lurch. Had she wanted more? Did she want to be his? But the sadness disappeared from her eyes and her expression turned sultry. Wishful thinking was making him see things that weren't there.

She slid around him and crawled to the middle of the bed, giving him a tantalizing view of her round ass. His chest rose and fell with increasing speed. When she reached the head of the bed, she turned around and beckoned him with the crook of her finger. He jumped to his feet and kicked off his jeans faster than he'd ever moved before. He was on top of her so quickly that she gasped in surprise, her eyes wide and a little intimidated.

The grin that spread across his face felt predatory, but when he leaned down to kiss her, his touch was tender…reverent. She had gifted him with a part of herself tonight. Her music still sang through his veins. Even as his kiss grew hungrier, more frantic, he saw the extraordinary woman in his arms and she deserved nothing less than his reverence.

"Daniel." When he drew back to stare down into her eyes, she cupped his cheek in her hand. "Claim me."

Her words awoke a primal need in him that he'd been trying to subdue. His hand found her center, wet and hot. She was ready for him, but he wanted her to feel as wild as he felt. His thumb drew lazy circles over her nub and she moaned, writhing under him.

"Do you want me?" he asked, inserting a finger into her tight warmth.

Her back arched off the bed. "Yes."

"Yes, what?" He added a second finger and she whimpered.

"I want you." She jerked frantically against his hand. "I want you inside of me."

"I am inside of you." He drew his fingers out and pushed them even deeper inside her. Tremors were running down his spine and sweat dripped down his forehead. Even as he teased her, he knew he couldn't hold back much longer.

"Please."

The raw need in her single word broke his control, and he spread her legs wide and tilted her hips up to receive him. The pleasure that coursed through him when he pushed into her was so intense that it almost felt like pain. He held still to gather himself, but Megan wiggled against him impatiently.

"Please." It was his turn to plead. "If you keep doing that, this isn't going to last very long."

"I don't need long." She moved against him again. "I promise."

True to her words, she fell apart with his name on her lips as he buried himself inside her and rode her with wild, hard thrusts. And as she clenched around him, his own climax wrenched a guttural cry out of him and waves of pleasure wracked through him. When the real world settled around him again, he moved his weight off her and collapsed beside her.

God, she was beautiful. Her face was flushed a delicate pink, and tendrils of hair clung to her damp forehead, but it was the sweet tenderness in her eyes that made his heart perform a somersault. He reached out to tuck her hair behind her ear. He wanted nothing more than to keep her by his side and wake up with her in the morning. *Every morning.* He snatched his hand away from her. The greedier he became, the more it would hurt when this ended—because everything ended…at least for him. The thought washed away his lethargy as effectively as a bucket of ice water.

"Let me take you home," he said curtly and rolled out of bed. But not before he saw the hurt in her eyes. This time, he knew he hadn't imagined it. Still, he did nothing about it…because he was a coward.

Eleven

For every step Megan took toward Daniel, he seemed to take two steps back. The night he gave her the Stradivarius, he'd turned brusque and distant after they made love—just like their second night together. Both nights, it felt as though he was kicking her out of his place. Like he couldn't wait to be alone.

He'd told her that he had emotional baggage and it wasn't about her, but it was hard not to feel hurt by it. Especially when all she wanted to do was fall asleep in his arms and wake up next to him so they would be the first thing the other saw in the morning.

A forlorn sigh slipped past her lips as she stood waiting behind the curtains with her sisters. Thankfully, the Chamber Orchestra was performing onstage, so her sisters didn't hear her. She wished she could spill her guts to them so they could help her figure out what to do, but that wasn't an option. She refused to add another secret for them to keep from their father. It wasn't fair to her sisters.

Besides, Megan already knew what she had to do to win Daniel's heart. She would have to take three steps forward every time he took two steps back. She would back him into a corner and love him relentlessly until he was hers. She wouldn't dwell on how much it stung every time he pushed her away. He had a gentle, kind soul. It would hurt him to know that he caused her pain.

And she instinctively understood that he was distancing himself from her to protect himself—from what, she didn't know yet. Maybe a part of it had to do with his unhappy childhood. She sighed again. It was hard to figure everything out when he shared so little of his past with her.

"We're on, girls." Angie nodded at them with her game face on.

"Let's go have some fun," Chloe said with a cheeky grin and strode out onto the stage first.

Megan followed her with a smile, reminded of what a privilege it was to play with her sisters. They were such amazing musicians and she loved them more than words. As long as she had them—and their music—by her side, she could take anything life threw her way. The thought sounded too much like she was preparing to lose Daniel. No, she wasn't going to let herself give up so easily.

Her unsettled thoughts spilled into her music at

times, but her sisters caught her and lifted her up before it could affect their performance. Knowing they had her back and they deserved nothing less than her best, Megan was able to give her one-hundred-percent for the rest of the performance and finished strong.

After bowing to thundering applause, they walked off the stage and Megan breathed a sigh of relief.

Angie put her hand on her back and said softly, "Are you feeling okay, Megan?"

"I'm fine. The doctor said it was normal to have trouble concentrating sometimes." She shrugged as nonchalantly as she could manage. "Pregnancy brain."

"Hmm." Her older sister didn't buy it for a second and gave her a penetrating gaze. "You know I'm always here for you, right?"

"Right," Megan said without hesitation. She knew without a doubt that her sister would always be there for her—would always help shoulder any burden she carried. Even so—or maybe because of that—she had to carry this one on her own. "I know, so stop worrying."

"Okay," Chloe answered instead of Angie. She'd been standing beside them, quietly listening to the whole conversation. "We'll stop worrying for now, but we're going to swoop in the minute we feel like you're in trouble."

"Fair enough." Megan grinned at her sisters. "God, I love you guys so much. I can't stand it."

"Can I join you three and bask in the warmth of sisterly love?" Joshua came to stand with his arms around Angie's and Megan's shoulders.

He leaned down and kissed the top of her older sister's head, and Megan could swear he breathed in the scent of her hair, his eyes fluttering closed for a moment. The love between Angie and Joshua seemed to cocoon them in a sphere of shimmering light. All she wanted was a love like theirs. Megan nibbled her bottom lip as wistful envy swept through her. Suddenly, she missed Daniel with an urgency that nearly brought tears to her eyes.

"You're always welcome to join us," Angie said, snuggling into Joshua's side.

They all turned when someone cleared his throat behind them. Daniel stood a few steps away with three elegant bouquets of calla lilies in his arms. "I hope I'm not intruding."

"Of course you're not." Megan restrained herself from throwing herself into his arms, but there wasn't a damn thing she could do about the giant smile that spread across her face. "I didn't know you were coming."

"I want to kick myself for not attending your concerts sooner. I've been missing out," he said ruefully. "You ladies are extraordinary and it was a privilege hearing you play tonight."

The Han sisters simultaneously blushed with pleasure. Even Angie—with the love of her life standing right next to her—wasn't immune to Daniel's brand of sincerity and charm. They each took the bouquet he held out to them and beamed at him.

"You must be Daniel Pak." Joshua straightened to his full, imposing height and drew his wide shoulders back. His voice could've frozen a lake as he said, "I'm Joshua Shin, Megan's brother-in-law."

"It's a pleasure to meet you," Daniel said evenly, extending his hand.

Joshua narrowed his eyes and paused for two seconds before shaking Daniel's hand. "I'm afraid I can't say the same."

"Joshua!" Angie slapped her husband's arm before turning to Daniel. "Please don't mind him. He's just protective of my younger sisters."

"Come on, Hyungbu," Chloe said with a cringe. "You're embarrassing us."

Deciding her brother-in-law was chastised enough, Megan met Daniel's slightly bemused gaze and shrugged. Glancing around to make sure there was no one close enough to overhear, she said, "That's what you get for knocking me up."

After a stunned second, Daniel and her sisters burst out laughing, dispelling any lingering awkwardness. Even Joshua couldn't hang on to his scowl as he said, "I guess Megan doesn't need me to look out for her."

"No, she doesn't," Daniel said with obvious pride. "I'm no match for her."

"Now that we can all agree on that," Megan said hurriedly when her sisters glanced between her and Daniel with speculative expressions, "should we go out for a nightcap?"

"That sounds like a great—" Joshua began. Angie leaned close to him and whispered something in his ear, and his eyes bulged slightly. He cleared his throat.

"It seems Angie and I have a prior engagement. We'll take a raincheck on that nightcap."

"And I have to work on some slides for a presentation tomorrow," Chloe moaned. "It's so hard balancing my duties as a professional musician with my duties as a grad student."

Megan raised an eyebrow. That was an elaborate explanation to simply bow out of a casual get-together. "So what you're saying is that you plan on staying up all night playing League of Legends again?"

"Precisely." Chloe grinned unrepentantly, then she suddenly scowled. "I'm hoping to run into my arch nemesis tonight so I can kick his ass."

"You have an arch nemesis on League of Legends?" Daniel asked with a broad smile. He probably thought her younger sister was as cute as a button, because she really was.

"Yes," Chloe hissed. "I. Hate. Him."

"All right. Settle down," Angie said wryly. "Save that antagonism for the game. You're scaring Daniel."

Which wasn't quite true. In fact, he looked absolutely delighted. He seemed to truly enjoy interacting with her siblings. A pang of sadness ran through Megan as she remembered the lonely childhood he'd had.

"Megan, may I give you a lift home?" Daniel said with impeccable politeness, but there was a glint in his eyes that made her pulse spike.

"Yes, I'd appreciate that, since my sisters are abandoning me," she replied with forced nonchalance.

When it was finally just the two of them as they

walked to his car, he took her hand and placed a lingering kiss on the inside of her wrist. "I'm actually relieved I got you to myself."

"Are you now?" The kiss left her a little breathless.

He pushed her up against the passenger door of his car. "I could still feel your music pulsing through my veins. You were magnificent and I feel...frantic."

"Frantic?" she squeaked inelegantly. She could feel his hard length pressing into her stomach.

"Like I would go mad if I don't have you soon," he growled, his lips a breath away from hers.

She closed the remaining distance between them and kissed him with a moan, burying her hands in his hair. She wanted to be everything to him...his love, his family...if only he'd let her. Loving him in secret hurt so much. A sob escaped her before she could push it down.

Daniel pulled back and held her face between his hands. "Megan, what's wrong?"

Her chest rose and fell so quickly she felt light-headed, and for a second—just a split second—she was tempted to tell him everything. That she loved him. That she wanted them to be a family. But the moment passed because she couldn't risk losing him. Not yet.

"We should take this to someplace more private." She couldn't quite manage a smile. "We can't risk starting any rumors that might reach my father's ears. We're so close to having the board members' support secured."

His eyes bore into hers as though he saw through

her half-truth, but he merely nodded and opened the car door for her. They drove in silence to his place, their moods subdued. Megan felt his sidelong glances on her, but she stared out the window, not having the energy to pretend everything was okay.

As it stood, what they had between them wouldn't last. No matter how carefully she treaded. So did she want to risk their arrangement for a chance at something real? Something lasting? *Yes*. They would always be in each other's lives in some capacity, because of the baby, but the thought of being cordial acquaintances made her heart bleed. What hurt the most was that it wouldn't be much different from what they were now—casual lovers.

She finally turned away from the window and met Daniel's searching gaze. He reached for her hand and she linked her fingers through his. Megan knew herself. She couldn't settle for anything less than all-consuming love. If she lost him trying to win his love, then at least she would know that she went down fighting. She would have no regrets.

Last night, Megan had made love to him with such tenderness and generosity that Daniel had felt humbled and honored. Then, why did he feel so unsettled? Because it had felt like goodbye. She'd made love to him as though it was for the last time.

He drew several deep breaths through his nose but couldn't fill up his lungs. He listlessly flipped through the documents on his desk before shoving them aside. Leaning back in his chair, he spun around to face the windows of his office. It was past eight and the city below twinkled with lights. But the stunning view looked bleak to his eyes tonight. He spun back to his desk and picked up his cell phone.

Daniel hadn't heard from Megan all day. Even though he'd reached for his device countless times throughout the day, he couldn't work up the nerve to text her himself. He almost dropped his cell when it buzzed in his hand. His breath left him in a whoosh when he saw that it was Megan.

I'm finally cashing in on your offer.

His eyebrows drew together as he typed back.

What offer?

Her response was immediate.

I'm dying for some tiramisu and pistachio cannoli.

Daniel threw back his head and laughed, relief rolling through him. Everything was fine. They were fine.

Where should I deliver them to? Should I park a couple blocks from your house and text you?

He tapped his foot as she typed her response.

I would like front door delivery please. Mrs. Chung is visiting her daughter and won't be back till tomorrow afternoon. And as you know, my father is in Austin for business. Maybe I'll even let you come inside.

Daniel grabbed his jacket and headed out with his heart pounding. He couldn't wait to see Megan. He'd seen her the night before, but that felt like an eternity ago. If he sounded lovesick, he decided not to notice it. And she was alone tonight. Maybe he would get to wake up with her in the morning. The thought didn't plunge him into a blind panic anymore—the *want* far outweighed the fear. He broke into a run to reach his car.

Besides, it didn't mean anything. He was only curious to see what she looked like waking up in the morning. Everything about her would be warmed and softened by sleep—her cheeks rosy, her lips full and parted, her silken hair tousled around her bare shoulders. He would kiss her awake. First, on her shoulder, then at the hollow below her throat, then her eyes— one then the other—and finally her lips, which would blossom into a smile underneath his before she opened her eyes. And he would be the first person she saw in the new day. He wanted that—desperately—even though wanting more would do him no good.

He picked up the tiramisu and cannoli from an Italian restaurant nearby. It was fancy, expensive and close. The food wasn't as good as the hole-in-the-wall Italian restaurant in his old neighborhood in New York, but it would have to do. He had to remind himself to ease off the gas pedal several times as he rushed to Megan's house. Getting a ticket would take up more time than his speeding would save.

Out of habit, he parked his car a block away and walked to her front door. He rang the doorbell and waited for Megan with blood pounding in his ears. He was being ridiculous, but he was too happy to care. When the door finally opened, the smile she gave him almost convinced him that she was as happy to see him as he was to see her.

"Your delivery is here," he said, holding up the bag of dessert.

"Thank God." She pretended to sag against the door, then stepped back to let him in. "What are you standing around for? Off you go to the kitchen."

She led the way and he followed a few steps behind to admire the view. She was in a silky pink pajama set that slid across her skin as she walked in front of him, hips swaying. She probably put them on for comfort but she looked sexy as hell to him. He wondered if he could have her before they had the dessert.

She looked over her shoulder, opening her mouth to say something, but whatever she saw in his expression made her blush and she turned back without saying a word. When they were in the kitchen, she scooted to the far end of the room, putting the island between them. He took a predatory step toward her and she pressed herself against the counter, holding up a hand.

"Dessert first," she said, sounding breathless.

He continued stalking toward her and she watched him with her hands clenched on the edge of the counter, her chest rising and falling rapidly. His eyes lazily slid down her body, then back up to her face. He stopped inches away from her and placed his hands over hers, trapping her between his arms and his hard, aching body.

"Define *dessert*," he purred, drawing his nose down the side of her face. Her shuddering breath made him smile. His hands circled her waist and he hefted her onto the counter. Spreading her legs, he stepped in between them.

The shyness melted away from Megan as she stared into his eyes and she smoothed her hands over his chest, then over his shoulders. "Dessert is something… decadent. A sweet, rich indulgence. Something that makes you feel a little…sinful."

He crushed his mouth against hers like a man starved. He wanted her so much that a sob lodged itself in his chest. He moaned her name against her lips, which parted for him in invitation. Their tongues slithered against each other, tasting and teasing, and his body caught fire. His need for her was consuming him and he wanted her to burn for him.

But he froze when a sharp gasp escaped her. Both her hands flew to her stomach and her head dropped. Even though her breathing was ragged, she sat still and silent. Fear sliced through his lust-fogged mind.

"God, Megan." He grabbed her shoulders and ducked his head to catch her expression. Was she in pain? "Tell me what's wrong, sweetheart."

"Oh, Daniel. There's nothing wrong. The opposite actually." She raised her tearstained face at last. "It's the baby. He moved. I felt him move."

His knees turned liquid with relief. She was okay. Thank God, she was okay. Then goose bumps rose on his arms as he registered what she had said. The baby—their baby—moved.

"Can I...?" He cleared his throat and tried again, "Do you think I could feel him?"

"Well, let's see." Megan tugged his hand onto her stomach and lowered her head again, as though listening to her body. "It's very subtle. Almost like bubbles rising to the surface."

They both held their breaths and waited. Nothing happened for a minute and Daniel was about to withdraw his hand when he felt it...felt him. The softest fluttering against his palm. He gasped and stepped back, his arm dropping to his side. "Was...was that him?"

"Yes." Happy tears filled Megan's eyes once more. "That's him."

He gingerly placed his hand on Megan's stomach again, and the baby tickled it. "Hi, there."

"Say hi to Daddy," Megan whispered, gazing down at her stomach—her hand placed over his.

The baby fluttered again as though he heard his mother's urging. Heat gathered behind Daniel's eyes and undefinable emotions clogged his throat. Something between a laugh and a sob escaped from him. Then he laughed again because he was so damn happy.

Megan joined in his laughter, tears sliding down her face. He swiped his thumbs across her cheeks and pressed his forehead against hers. Their laughter died down and their breathing evened out as they leaned against each other. Something peaceful and content stole into his heart. This moment. He would never forget this perfect moment for the rest of his life.

"Megan? What…?" He spun around at the sound of Mr. Han's voice, and the older man's eyes widened with shock. "Daniel?"

Daniel's hand was still pressed against Megan's stomach. He didn't remember doing so but he had wrapped a protective arm around her and had pulled her close. She was trembling against him and he tightened his hold on her, cursing under his breath. He couldn't let Megan bear the brunt of her father's anger and disappointment. He had to shield her from it somehow. But how?

"Appa—" Megan's voice shook and when her father held up his hand, she pressed her lips together.

"Are you seeing my daughter, Daniel?" Mr. Han leveled a steely gaze at him.

"Yes, sir," he said. There would be no more lies from this point on. He felt Megan turn to stare at him.

"How long has this been going on?" His mentor's frown smoothed out and hope stole into his expression. *God.* Daniel felt guilt twist in his gut.

"About two months, sir," he answered past his dry throat.

"Two months? So is this the result of my stellar matchmaking skills?" Mr. Han's face split into a full-blown grin as he regarded the two of them. Then his expression turned somber again. "And you are at peace with the fact that my daughter is pregnant with another man's child?"

Daniel felt Megan stiffen beside him and he turned to meet her gaze. She must have seen the grim determination on his face because she slowly shook her head and gripped his hand. She'd worked so hard to protect him from her father's wrath. He gave her a small smile and smoothed back a strand of hair from her eyes.

"Mr. Han—" Daniel looked at his mentor and friend "—Megan is pregnant with my child. I am the baby's father."

Minsung Han staggered back two steps, the shock, betrayal and hurt plain on his face. Megan scrambled down from her perch on the counter and stepped toward her father with her hand outstretched. Mr. Han drew himself up and pointed a warning finger at her.

"Stay where you are. I don't want to hear a word out of you," her father grit out in an uncompromising tone before he turned to Daniel. "As for you... I presume you wouldn't have kept the baby's parentage a secret—making a mockery out of me—if you intended to marry her."

It wasn't posed as a question, so Daniel said nothing. He didn't say that he would marry his daughter in a hot second if only she would have him, but she'd made it abundantly clear that she didn't want to marry him. Because...because she wanted to marry for love. He couldn't...give her that. If he loved her and lost her, then everything would be tainted...even his love for his son. Something inside him began quaking.

"Appa, please listen," Megan tried again.

"Not. A. Word," he roared.

"Do *not* speak to her that way." Daniel stepped forward, half shielding Megan from her father's rage.

Minsung Han's face transformed into a mask of indifference and he waved a dismissive hand toward Daniel. "You have one week to tender your resignation."

They stood in a cocoon of shock as the sound of Mr. Han's footsteps faded away. Then Megan took a shuddering breath as though she was waking up from a nightmare.

"Daniel, it's going to be okay," she said urgently. "I...I just have to tell my father that you proposed to me—that you tried to do the right thing—but I said no."

"Then we proceeded to see each other behind his back and didn't tell him that I was the baby's father. We lied to him, Megan," he reminded her gently.

"No, I could explain everything. I'll make him listen." Megan hugged her arms around her midriff. "I'll make him understand."

The only way to appease her father—and to protect Megan from his anger—was for them to get married. His stomach dropped to his feet. He had to ask her... even if she said no again. He had to try.

"Megan, marry me," he said, wrapping his hands around her shoulders. "Marry me. Please."

She raised stunned eyes to his and searched his face. Her voice shook when she asked, "Do you...? Do you love me?"

"Love?" Something inside him seemed to shrivel. He dropped his hands to his sides and took a step back from her. "I told you that I...I couldn't give you the fantasy. This isn't a fairy tale, Megan. What we have is enough. We have a child between us. We respect and enjoy each other. And I will never be unfaithful to you. I promise you that. Isn't that enough?"

A light in her eyes seemed to flicker and die, and a voice inside him screamed. *Coward.* Her bottom lip trembled and she bit viciously down on it. He wanted to reach out and pull her into his arms—hold on tight to her. She breathed in and out of her nose until the trembling eased. She drew back her shoulders, then lifted her chin.

"No, that isn't enough." Quiet strength resonated from her. "I won't marry you, Daniel, because I deserve to be loved. I deserve the fairy tale."

He wanted to shout and rant that fairy tales end. That love was a fickle emotion that faded, leaving pain in its wake. But he said nothing as he watched her walk out of the kitchen and disappear down the hallway. Because even though he had protected himself from the destructive force of love, pain had still found him. Even though he'd known that it was inevitable that she would leave him—abandon him—he still felt himself breaking apart into pieces.

And he said to no one in particular, "But *I* don't deserve to be loved."

Twelve

Megan knocked on her dad's bedroom door, but there was no answer. It might be for the best. She could hardly stand on her own, and her teeth were chattering so hard that her dad wouldn't be able to understand a word out of her. So, leaning against the hallway wall, she dragged herself to her room with halting, faltering steps.

She half fell onto her bed and curled into herself. Her head and limbs were heavy, and she felt like she was sinking deeper and deeper into the mattress. She imagined herself being swallowed up by it along with her loss and sorrow.

An odd numbness had come over her as she'd walked away from Daniel. She didn't know how long it would last—how long it would keep the pain at bay. Anxiety crept into her. She felt like a rabbit being hunted as she hid from the inevitable grief. She jolted up and scrambled back into the headrest, pulling the covers up to her chin. Her breathing grew ragged. She didn't want to face what she'd done. She couldn't face it.

Was he gone? Had he left? Maybe if she ran back downstairs, she'd find him in the kitchen, standing exactly where she'd left him. Then she could tell him that she would marry him. That she would take whatever he could offer her. That she didn't need his love as long as she had some part of him.

What was it he'd said? Ah, yes. She would have his respect and fidelity. That was something. And their passion. There was that. But how long could passion burn without love? An image of their cold marriage bed, where they slept with their backs turned toward each other, flashed through her mind. She shivered and pulled the covers more tightly around her.

Then the baby fluttered in her stomach as though he was saying, "And me. There's me." Yes, they would have their baby. The tears she'd been holding at bay finally started to fall. Would Daniel love their son? She knew he would—that he already did. And how long would it be before Megan began resenting their little boy for having his love—the love that he denied her?

The tears fell faster as sobs wracked her body. It would destroy her to marry Daniel knowing he didn't love her. Her love for him would turn into poison inside her and she would become a bitter shadow of herself. She would lose herself forever. No, she couldn't let that happen. She couldn't do that to her father, her sisters and her baby. She couldn't do that to herself.

So she had to let Daniel go…no matter how much it hurt. Her sobs turned into wails that ravaged her throat, and she clawed at her chest. It was only when her dad wrapped his arms around her and tucked her under his chin that she realized he had come into her room. She wailed until her voice became a husky rasp, then she sobbed until her body went limp with fatigue, and she cried until her tears dried up—until she was empty.

Her dad held her tight against his chest even after she stilled and grew silent. He held her until exhaustion claimed her and darkness edged into her consciousness. At last, in the safety of his arms, Megan allowed herself to fall into a dreamless slumber where she could stop hurting for a little while.

Megan woke up early next morning with her throat raw and her eyes swollen. She knew the damage outside was far less evident than the mangled mess that was her shattered heart. Even so, she pushed back her covers and got out of bed. She showered, dried her hair and dressed in a cozy sweater and comfortable leggings. She had to show her dad that she was okay— that she was going to be okay. It must've broken his heart to watch her fall apart last night even after she'd betrayed him in the worst possible way.

She went downstairs to the kitchen and puttered around to make some tea and toast. Once everything was finished and arranged on a tray, she carried it upstairs and stopped in front of her dad's door.

"Appa, I need you to open the door me," she said, her voice husky but steady. "My hands are full."

The door opened, and her dad's eyes roamed her face for a moment before he stepped back to let her in. He was dressed casually in a pair of khakis and a polo shirt with a cardigan over it. He was planning on staying home—she swallowed a lump in her throat—to look after her.

Megan placed the tray on the coffee table in the sitting area and sat down in one of the armchairs. "Mrs. Chung will be back this afternoon. For now, you'll have to make do with toast."

With a noncommittal grunt, he settled into the chair next to her and spread his toast with a generous pat of butter and strawberry jam. He took a big bite before pouring tea into both their cups. She followed his example and munched on some toast even though she couldn't taste a thing. She took a sip of her tea to help her swallow it down.

"Thank you," she said quietly. "I know I've hurt you. You didn't deserve that. I'm going to apologize for that in a minute. But more than anything, I want to thank you. Thank you for holding me together last night. I don't know what I would've done without you."

"You don't ever have to wonder what you will do without me." He gazed steadily at her. "Because I will always be there for you."

"I know." She sniffed and shook her head. If she

started crying again, she didn't know if she could ever stop. "I love you, Daddy."

"I know."

"And now, we've come to the portion of the program where I grovel," she said with a nervous laugh. "I'm sorry I lied to you. I'm so sorry I hurt you."

"You made a fool out of me." His expression turned thunderous in an instant as though he'd been suppressing his rage until he knew she was okay. He rose from his seat and paced with short, agitated steps. "To think I was trying to set you two up."

"I thought I had good reason to keep things from you, but now all those reasons seem nonsensical." She threw her hands up in a helpless gesture.

"There is no excuse for what you did," he said in a low, furious voice.

"You're right. I should have told you the truth as soon as I found out."

"What?" Her dad's eyebrows rose in surprise. He sat back down and wiped his hand over his face. "You didn't know all along?"

"I'm sure you don't want to hear this again, but I really did have a one-night stand with a stranger," she said, swallowing her mortification. "When I found out I was pregnant, I had no way of contacting him. That's all true. It doesn't make what I did okay, but I never told you an outright lie."

"Yes, it doesn't make what you did okay," he snapped, but some of the anger seemed to have seeped out of him. He jerked his chin toward her. "So tell me what happened."

"I didn't know who Daniel was…until that night you invited him over for dinner."

He huffed an incredulous laugh then stared at her with wide eyes. "Wait. You're serious."

"Yes. Imagine my surprise running into my one-night stand—three months after the fact—in my own house."

"And you had another surprise for him…"

"Daniel must have been shocked, but he asked me to marry him the moment I told him I was pregnant. I'm the one who refused him. He wanted to tell you everything, but I convinced him not to."

Megan explained her brilliant plan to win over the board members so her dad wouldn't react rashly to the news. "Daniel wanted to be in the baby's life and didn't want to risk having to relocate far away from me and the baby."

"Thank you for thinking so highly of me," her dad muttered.

"You can't say I was wrong," she said gently. "You asked him for his resignation last night. Remember?"

"I remember." He sat up in his chair. "And I'm standing by my decision."

"But Appa…" He raised an imperious hand and she snapped her mouth shut. She wasn't there to ask him for a favor. She was there to beg for his forgiveness. "Just please remember that I'm the one who refused to marry him. He…he even asked me again last night…and…and I…"

"That's all right. You don't need to continue." He

sighed. "I can guess what you said from your state. Tell me, Megan. Why did you say no?"

"Because…" she choked out as every raw crack in her broken heart burned. She closed her eyes to gather herself. "Because I want to marry for love."

"I think," he said quietly, "you *would* be marrying for love."

For a moment, all she could do was blink at her dad. "Am I that obvious?"

"A person doesn't grieve like you did yesterday unless they lost someone they loved." He understood. He'd grieved so deeply when her mom died.

"I do love Daniel—" Megan took a shuddering breath "—but he doesn't love me."

"Are you sure about that? The scene I walked in on last night…" Her dad arched an eyebrow. "You two were drowning in each other's eyes and glowing with happiness. Hell, that sounds like poetry and I'm no poet. There's just no other way to describe what I saw."

"He thinks love is a fantasy…" she said uncertainly, her heart pounding with a terrifying glimmer of hope.

"For a smart man, he does a great job of acting the fool." He clucked his tongue. "Have you told him that you loved him?"

"No." She had planned to tell him. "I… I was afraid of pushing him away."

"Have you ever considered the possibility that he was scared, too?" her dad asked. "Maybe he was afraid that you don't feel the same way—so afraid that he couldn't even admit to himself that he loved you."

"That's just wild speculation," she whispered, but she couldn't dismiss what he'd said. She didn't want to.

"More like an educated guess." He wagged his finger at her. "I know what I saw. Credit your old man with some wisdom. I've lived a lot longer than you have."

She suddenly couldn't talk about Daniel—or even think about him—for another second. She stood from her chair and kissed her dad's cheek. "Thank you, Appa."

"And don't think I've forgiven you, yet," he said as though he meant "you're forgiven."

Megan carried the half-empty tray back to the kitchen, not sure how to feel…not sure she wanted to feel anything at all. Now that she'd made the first step toward making things right with her dad, the guilt that had kept the devastation at bay diminished, and even her determination to appear okay seemed to dwindle.

She shuffled into the living room and lay down on the couch and curled into a ball—or as much as her growing stomach would allow. She did nothing to stop the tears that dripped down from the corners of her eyes until the hair on her temple became damp with them. Her eyelids became too heavy to keep open so she closed them, not caring she'd only just woken up.

In the end, she hadn't fought for Daniel—for them. She'd completely chickened out. So much for being brave and courageous. Her courage had deserted her when everything had been on the line. She'd been too scared to tell him that she loved him. Even so…

he'd let her walk away. A sob tore through her throat. Couldn't he have fought for her just a little?

Even if her dad was right, she couldn't risk getting her heart broken for a second time by confessing her love to him. At least, not yet. She needed time to heal—needed time to grow strong again. Only then would she know if she had the courage to fight for him.

Daniel hadn't slept or eaten but he'd consumed quite a bit of whiskey. He was late for work—soon to be his former job—but he stood under the spray of steaming hot water to wash away the stench of alcohol seeping out of his pores. Effectively fired or not, he respected Jigu Corporation too much to go into the office looking—and smelling—like the wreck he was.

He told himself what a close call that had been. If he was like this now, how would he have been if he'd let himself fall in love with Megan? There would've been nothing left of him if he'd lost her after he fell for her. Laughter snuck out of him and echoed hollowly in the shower. His shoulders shook with the force of the laugh and he leaned against the wall for support. When he realized he sounded hysterical, he shut his mouth and clenched his teeth to stop laughing.

He needed to get to the office. He had a week to tie up loose ends and streamline the transition for his successor. Stepping out of the shower, he dried off briskly and wiped his hand across the fogged-up mirror. He scowled at the image staring back at him. He needed a shave, but he couldn't stand looking at himself a moment longer, so he turned around and walked into his room. He carelessly pulled clothes off the hanger and rushed to dress himself. He was desperate to get out of his penthouse, away from his own company. He had to lose himself in his work.

Once he got to Jigu, he nodded curtly to his assistant, making her cheery smile slide off her face, and locked himself in his office. First thing first, he wrote his resignation letter. After typing and deleting a half dozen drafts, he decided to go with the first version he'd written: *Please accept my resignation...* Bland, generic and completely inadequate to express the remorse he felt for what he'd done to Minsung Han.

He printed out the letter, folded it with crisp, sharp edges and inserted it into a pristine white envelope. Then he held and stared at it for God knew how long before he picked up the phone and dialed Mr. Han's extension. No answer. Daniel called the CEO's executive assistant.

"Is Mr. Han in?" he asked more brusquely than he'd intended.

"No, Mr. Pak," she said with cool professionalism. "He said he will be working from home this morning. He might come in late afternoon, but he said to cancel all meetings for today."

Daniel hung up the phone with a mumbled thank-you and stood from his chair. Jigu Corporation's CEO never worked from home and never canceled meetings at the last minute. He wore his professionalism like an armor and sought to be an example for all his employees. No matter how shocked and betrayed he might've been the night before, Mr. Han would not stay home to sulk or lick his wounds.

Megan. Something must be wrong with Megan. Daniel paced back and forth, clenching and unclenching his hands. It couldn't be the baby. The baby was healthy and moving… His mind flashed back to the kitchen and the joy he'd felt in that moment. He closed his eyes and shook his head. He couldn't think about that. He was certain he wouldn't be able to survive dwelling on that moment because it would remind him of what he'd lost. No, the baby was fine. But Megan… maybe she wasn't fine.

Try as he might, he couldn't forget the pain in her eyes when he all but told her that he didn't love her. She would get over it, wouldn't she? They'd both agreed that there wouldn't be any promises. She had to have known that the affair would eventually end. Hadn't she? She would've been the one to leave him. Like they all do. In fact, she *was* the one who'd ended things. She was the one who'd refused to marry him— the one who'd walked away from him.

He cringed with shame. That was a new low for him. He knew exactly what he was doing when he'd told her that what they had was enough—that he couldn't give her the *fantasy.* He was the one who ended their relationship. He was the one who had hurt her. *God, please let Megan be okay.*

To hang on to his sanity, he threw himself into his work. He went from one project to the next, document after document, barking out orders to anyone who might slow him down. He had to keep moving.

When his phone buzzed, he nearly growled, "Yes?"

"Mr. Han would like to see you in his office," Terri said quietly.

He gripped his phone and took a deep breath. "Let him know I'll be there shortly. Thank you."

Daniel raked his fingers through his hair and stood up. He put on his suit jacket and slid his resignation letter into the inside pocket before walking out of his office. He offered a small smile to his assistant as a meager apology for being an asshole all day, then made his way to the CEO's office.

"I'm here to see Mr. Han," Daniel said to the executive assistant.

"Yes, please go right in," she said with a gracious nod.

After a courtesy knock, he walked into the CEO's office, closing the door behind him. Mr. Han kept his eyes on the document he was reading until Daniel stood in front of his desk. When the older man finally met his eyes, he wished the CEO would resume reading. Daniel realized that he had never before seen what Minsung Han looked like when he was regarding an adversary.

Mr. Han's gaze was both ice and fire and 100 percent intimidating. Not that Daniel couldn't hold his own against intimidation, but he was in no position to stare the CEO down. He was there to grovel to salvage whatever he could of his relationship with his mentor, which couldn't be much. But he had to try.

"Here is my letter of resignation." Daniel held out the envelope, but Minsung Han made no move to take it from him. After an awkward, silent stretch of time, Daniel finally placed his resignation letter on the desk. "I know an apology doesn't mean much at this point, but I still want to offer you my deepest, sincerest apology. I have no excuse for deceiving you…"

"And you have an excuse for impregnating my daughter?" Mr. Han barked.

"I didn't know who she was…" Daniel clamped his mouth shut on the excuse. "No, I have no excuse for that either."

"So you don't want to marry my daughter?"

"No, sir. That's not true. I want to marry her." He swallowed past a painful lump. "More than anything."

"Except you don't love her." Mr. Han's scowl inexplicably softened as he regarded Daniel. "At least, that's what Megan thinks."

"Is she… Is she okay?" He gripped the backs of the guest chairs in each hand as his blood pounded in his ears.

"No." Mr. Han's face closed off again. "She's not okay."

Daniel spun on his heels and took several steps toward the door before he stopped himself. Where was he going? To Megan? He couldn't go to her. He was the reason she wasn't okay. He returned to his spot in front of her father's desk.

"I'm sorry," Daniel said as something inside him cracked. He'd hurt Megan. He'd disappointed his mentor. "I'm going to take the week to get my projects in order and ready to hand off to my successor—"

"You think I could find your replacement in a

week?" Mr. Han scoffed. "Get out of my office. I don't want to look at your sorry face anymore. And take that damn envelope off my desk."

"But, sir—" Daniel frowned in confusion.

"I thought I told you to leave." The older man narrowed his eyes into menacing slits. "I also told you to take this with you. Do you think you can manage that?"

Daniel could only nod as he placed his resignation letter back in his jacket pocket. After bowing from his waist, he strode out of the CEO's office. Back at his desk, he spun his chair to face the window and stared unseeingly at the city below him.

There was no doubt that Mr. Han was furious with him. Even so, he'd refused to accept Daniel's resignation. What had changed his mind? He buried his head in his hands with a groan. Not what. Who. Megan must've told her father everything...down to the reason she'd refused his proposal. She had stood up for him even after he'd cast aside her love—

Daniel shot to his feet. *Her love.* Her answer to his proposal had depended on whether or not he loved her, because there was no doubt as to her love. *Do you love me?* He remembered her as she said those words—her eyes too wide for her face as hope and fear warred inside them. She loved him and all she needed to hear was that he loved her, too. She had given him the chance to have her—all of her—but he'd thrown it in her face.

He didn't remember what it felt like to be abandoned by his mother—he'd been too young—he only knew the bone-deep emptiness of her absence. But he did remember what it felt like to find the woman he thought he loved in the arms of his roommate. He remembered what it felt like to listen to Sienna tell him that she'd never wanted him…that he wasn't good enough for her.

Her betrayal had brought to surface the fear he'd carried with him all his life. That a boy his mother had abandoned—and his father didn't want—couldn't be good enough for anyone. He hated Sienna for that. He hated himself for that. The pain of that revelation had eaten away at him until he became someone who avoided commitment. A man who thought love was a fairy tale.

That was why he hadn't allowed himself fall in love with Megan—even though he'd known that it meant he would lose her. But having lost her, he realized the pain he felt when Sienna betrayed him was like a paper cut compared to the devastation he felt right now. With her, it was his pride that was injured, not his very soul.

And he'd used the baby as an excuse—a cover for his own fears. His love for his son would never falter. Even though he felt as though the world was crumbling down around him—on top of him—he could only feel joy that he would soon be a father. Nothing could change that.

He had let his wounded pride and bitterness rule his life. He'd let them blind him to the truth, but he was done with hiding—done with denying the greatest truth of his life. The reason he felt as though his heart was being torn into shreds was because he *had* fallen in love with Megan. He loved her with everything in him. But he had been too stubborn and too terrified to admit that he'd been wrong. Love was real. And maybe if an incredible woman like Megan loved him, then he *was* good enough.

What if it was too late? Fear clutched at him with its jagged claws, but he cast it aside. He had to right this wrong. There was no alternative. No matter what happened, he owed it to the baby to become the best man he could be—a man who fought for his mother's love. And he would strive to be good enough for Megan. He would do anything—risk any pain— to deserve her love.

But she was hurting. He couldn't demand to see her and pour out his heart to her when she couldn't possibly be ready to listen to him. He needed to give her time. As much as he could stand, which wasn't very much at all. He would try, though. Then he would tell her everything. He hoped to God it would be enough.

Thirteen

Megan walked into her ob-gyn's office alone, blinking back tears. There was no reason for her to cry. Even at the last prenatal appointment—even when they were together—she'd told Daniel that he didn't need to come to every one of them with her. But she hadn't seen him in over three weeks and missed him so much. That was still no excuse to ugly cry while peeing into a cup, so she didn't.

Besides, she had to focus on getting up the nerve to confess her love to Daniel and to build up some serious muscles around her heart so it wouldn't break if he said he didn't feel the same way about her. Because even if he didn't love her yet, she was willing to give him all the time he needed to fall in love with her. All he had to do was stop being so stubborn and accept that love was very real. And he would have to admit that, because she intended to show him how much she loved him every chance she got.

It was a great plan. It really was. But there was still the issue of lacking courage. Where had her nerve gone? She'd always thought she had plenty of pluck. But Daniel meant everything to her, and it was so hard to be brave when everything was on the line. She sighed. She was tired of all the circular thinking. She was just...tired.

After she provided the obligatory cup of pee, she came back out to the waiting room to sit until the nurse called her name. But Megan's steps faltered as she sucked in a long, sharp breath.

"Megan," Daniel murmured as he rose from his seat. His expression was carefully blank, but his eyes skimmed every inch of her with an intensity that made her insides tremble. She wasn't sure she would be able to put one foot in front of another so she stood where she'd stopped. "I can leave if you want me to."

She released the breath she'd been holding and walked up to him. "No, I want you to stay. The whole point of our debacle was to let you be a part of our child's life, every step of the way. No matter what happens, I still want that for you and the baby."

"For me and the baby." He nodded, his mouth settling into a grim line. "I... Thank you."

"Of course." She glanced at him uncertainly, wondering what she'd said to upset him.

"You should sit." With a gentle touch on her elbow,

he guided her to a chair and took the one next to her. "How…how are you?"

That was a loaded question. How would he react if she said, "Missing you? Trying to stay strong for the baby even though I want to curl up into a ball and cry most of the time?" In the end, she said what everyone always said whether it was true or not. "Fine."

He sighed and looked down at his hands, which were clenched into fists on top of his thighs. She felt like she was getting all her answers wrong. A touch of anger flared inside her. Why did he get to ask all the questions anyway?

"And how are you?" she asked, arching her eyebrow in challenge.

He raised his eyes to meet hers and the pain and longing in them took her breath away. He held her gaze as though to give her time to look inside of him—like he was laying himself bare for her. When he finally opened his mouth, she leaned toward him to hear his answer.

"Megan Han?" the nurse called from the doorway.

She wanted to snarl and tell the woman to piss off, but it wasn't the poor nurse's fault that she had shitty timing. Daniel stood first and held his hand out to her. She gingerly took it and allowed him to help her to her feet even though she could've gotten up on her own. She instinctively understood that *he* needed to help her.

"Hello, my dear." Dr. Pinkus walked into the examination room with her signature warm smile. "And Daniel."

"Hi, Dr. Pinkus," Megan said as Daniel nodded his hello.

"So, how have you been feeling?" the doctor asked.

"We felt the baby move," Megan whispered and Daniel stiffened by her side. That moment seemed like a lifetime ago. The joy and wonder that they'd shared remained crystal clear in her mind, but the memory of the sorrow that followed made her throat close up.

"Ah, the quickening." Dr. Pinkus nodded happily. "It's such a special moment."

"Yes," Daniel said thickly. "It was unforgettable."

Something in his voice made Megan turn sharply toward him, but he kept his eyes trained on the doctor as she explained the baby's growth and what to expect in the next four weeks. Megan nodded at the appropriate spots, but her mind was a mess of jumbled thoughts. Had Daniel been trying to tell her something before the nurse called her name? Was she imagining things that weren't there, because she wanted to? She didn't know. All she knew was that it hurt to see Daniel—to want him but not have him. It hurt too much.

They walked to the parking lot in silence, each lost in their own thoughts. Megan needed to get away from Daniel before she burst into tears. She didn't feel brave enough to fight for his love at the moment. She felt raw and scared.

"Thanks for coming today." She forced a stiff smile on her face. "I'll see you at the next appointment."

She'd opened the car door and moved to get inside when Daniel gripped her upper arm. "Megan."

She heard a world of emotions in that one word. He'd said her name as though his life depended on it. Her breath came in quick puffs. She couldn't... She pulled her arm out of his grasp and got inside her car.

"Bye, Daniel," she said without looking at him. He was holding the car door so she couldn't close it, and she felt panic building inside her. She was a second away from bursting when he finally let go and stepped back.

She shut the door and squealed out of the parking lot as the tears she'd been holding back rained down her cheeks.

Megan slept for three hours when she got home. She didn't feel like getting out of bed even when she woke up, but she had to get ready to meet her dad for dinner. The last thing she wanted to do was be out in public where there were people, but she couldn't refuse her dad. She had so much to make up to him.

After a long shower, she dried her hair to fall down in soft waves around her shoulders. She chose a rich yellow tunic dress to cheer herself up and added a soft pink lipstick to her light makeup. Getting herself ready for a dinner date with her dad made her feel a bit stronger, and she needed all the strength she could find.

The Italian restaurant her dad chose for dinner was one of her favorites and she found her lips curling into a smile as she walked inside. The interior was minimalistic with cream-colored walls and white linens, but the muted lights and lit candles on the tables gave the ambience a warm, inviting feeling.

"We have a reservation for two under Minsung Han," she told the host.

"Of course. Please follow me."

Her dad wasn't there yet, so she ordered herself a glass of iced tea and a basket of bread and butter. If he didn't come by the time she finished the bread, then she would text him. She was used to her dad running late for everything. Just like Daniel.

She didn't cringe away from the thought like she'd been doing for the past three weeks. She loved Daniel. Of course everything would remind her of him. It was time she accepted that and stopped trying to hide from her feelings. If she kept hiding, how was she going to win his love?

She asked for more butter as she worked her way through the bread basket. She glanced at her watch and decided to give her dad five more minutes before she texted him.

"Megan?"

She dropped the bread she was buttering on her plate and gaped at Daniel. "No."

"Pardon?" he asked, his eyebrows drawing together.

"No," she repeated. Her father has resumed his matchmaking scheme. "I can't believe he did this again."

She opened her purse and pulled out her phone to give her dad a piece of her mind. He knew she loved Daniel, and wanted to help—which was very sweet and all—but this was her life and he needed to stop meddling in it. But her dad had already texted her.

Sorry, my dear. I got detained at work. I hope you approve of your replacement date. She was so busy growling that she almost didn't hear Daniel. "Do you mind if I have a seat?"

"No, of course not. Please sit," she said, flustered. She took a deep breath through her nose and met Daniel's eyes. "I'm so sorry about my father."

"Are you kidding? Your father is amazing." He smiled sheepishly. "I'm going to buy him a drink. Well, depending on how things go tonight, I might even buy him a cellar full of drinks. Either way, I'm grateful to him."

"I'm sorry." Megan blinked. "I think I lost you."

"Never." All traces of a smile left Daniel's face. "You could never lose me."

"What?" He was staring at her with such unwavering focus that she forgot to breathe.

"You must hate me," he said with anguish in his voice.

She managed to shake her head.

"You couldn't wait to get away from me earlier today." He held up his hand. "Not that I blame you. You have every right to hate me."

"Stop saying that," she said with a confused frown. She didn't hate him. She loved him.

"Megan, I'm so sorry." He reached across the table as though he wanted to touch her but snatched his hand back at the last moment. "I'm sorry I couldn't tell you that I loved you. I'm sorry I let you walk away thinking we were finished."

She was shaking so badly that she had to clench her teeth to stop them from chattering. Hearing his apology made her realize how angry she'd been—at him and at herself. They had something special and precious, and they'd let it slip through their fingers.

"There was someone in college," he began. "I thought I was in love with her."

Her stomach dropped like rocks. She'd been right. He was in love with someone else. That was why he couldn't love her. Her nails dug into her palms.

"But she was only using me so she could get to my roommate," he stated matter-of-factly, as though it had happened to someone else.

She couldn't hold back her gasp. "That's horrible. I'm so sorry."

"She said I wasn't good enough." He paused for a second. "And I believed her. Deep down, I'd always believed that. Why else would my own mother abandon me?"

"Oh, Daniel. That's not true." She felt gutted. He didn't deserve that. Any of that. She reached for his hand and squeezed tight. "They were wrong. So very wrong. You are a good, kind man—deserving of love and loyalty."

"I know." He flipped her hand and linked his fingers through hers. "You showed me that."

"I'm not sure…"

"I…I thought that you would leave me, too." His

eyes searched her face. "I was so afraid I would lose you, too."

"What are you trying to tell me?" she asked, blood pounding in her ears.

"I'm trying to tell you that…I was wrong," he said. "Love isn't a fantasy. I know you love me."

She started and tried to jerk her hand out of his, but he held on tight.

"I'm sorry it took me so long to see that." He gazed at her with heartrending tenderness. "I was a fool for not realizing how fucking lucky I was."

She nodded her agreement because she didn't think her voice would work. A crooked grin touched his lips.

"I'm sorry it took me so long to realize that *I* love you," he said, his voice cracking at the end. "I love you, Megan. More than anything."

A choked sob broke free from her and still she couldn't say anything.

"Am I…? Am I too late?" he asked with such vulnerability that her heart broke a little. "Do you not love me anymore? No, that's okay. I'll win your love back. I'll do anything for you. All I want is a chance to love you. To show you that you are everything to me."

"Stop," she whispered.

"What?" There was stark fear on his face.

"Stop talking—" she took a shuddering breath "—and listen."

He nodded, holding her hand with both of his as though she might run away if he let go.

"I'm sorry, too," she said, tears sliding down her cheeks.

"No, you have nothing…"

"Daniel, listen."

He clamped his mouth shut and a muscle jumped in his jaw. She could see the effort it took him to wait for her to finish.

"I'm sorry I didn't fight for us. I loved you, but I was too afraid to tell you. I was scared of pushing you away." She bit down on her lower lip to stop it from shaking. "I should've been braver. I should've loved you more."

"You…*loved* me?" His Adam's apple bobbed as he struggled to swallow.

"I do love you still. So much," she said. "But what I'm trying to say is I'm sorry I didn't love you harder, because you deserve to be loved—to be loved with courage. You are…"

Daniel stood so quickly that his chair scraped across the floor, and she was in his arms before she could squeak in surprise.

"Stop talking," he said in a low, growly voice before his lips crushed against hers.

She didn't waste a second before she wrapped her arms around his neck and kissed him back with everything she had—all the love, all the passion, all the regret… No. No regret. There was no room for that.

A chuckle rumbled deep in his chest, which made her kiss him harder, but he gently but firmly pushed her away. "Megan."

She frowned and tried to tug him back. This time he laughed with his head thrown back. It was beautiful. He was beautiful. And she was going to make him do it all the time. She had a lifetime to make him laugh.

"We have to stop unless you want to be banned from this restaurant," he said. "Here, sit."

She lowered herself into the chair, but she wasn't happy about it. When Daniel sat back down across from her and pulled out his phone, she gave an outraged huff. "You dare look at your phone when you could be kissing me?"

He just smiled up at her and said, "I have to ask your father's permission for something. I'm not doing anything behind his back anymore. I really should do it in person, but I can't wait…"

"Daniel, you just confessed your undying love for me." He hadn't said anything about undying, but she was pretty sure it was implied. "I don't think now is the appropriate time for you to text with my father."

"Bear with me. It's very important." His phone buzzed right away as though her dad had been waiting for Daniel's text. He checked the message and laughed that happy laugh again. She wanted to bottle it and drink it up.

"What is going on?" she asked with a confused smile. Her eyes widened when Daniel got down on his knee and looked up at her. "Ohhh. Okay. I think I know what's going on."

"Megan Han." If she wasn't already in love with the man, she would've fallen for him when he gazed at her with such love and awe—as though it was a privilege for him to behold her. "Will you make me the happiest man alive by becoming my wife?"

"Do you love me?" she said in a shaky whisper.

"With all my heart," he answered without hesitation.

"Then, yes." She laughed even as tears spilled down her cheeks. "I'll marry you."

"Finally." He grinned as he leaned toward her.

She met him halfway but stopped a breath away from his lips. "All you needed were the magic words."

"I love you," he said as he claimed her lips and her heart.

She smiled smugly against his kiss. She knew her intuition wouldn't lead her astray. Daniel Pak was capable of love, deep and everlasting, and he was hers to love with all her heart.

* * * * *

#2923 ONE NIGHT RANCHER

The Carsons of Lone Rock • by Maisey Yates

To buy the property, bar owner Cara Thompson must spend one night at a ghostly hotel and asks her best friend, Jace Carson, to join her. But when forbidden kisses melt into passion, *both* are haunted by their explosive encounter...

#2924 A COWBOY KIND OF THING

Texas Cattleman's Club: The Wedding • by Reese Ryan

Tripp Nobel is convinced Royal, Texas, is perfect for his famous cousin's wedding. But convincing Dionna Reed, the bride's Hollywood best friend...? The wealthy rancher's kisses soon melt her icy shell, but will they be enough to tempt her to take on this cowboy?

#2925 RODEO REBEL

Kingsland Ranch • by Joanne Rock

With a successful bull rider in her bachelor auction, Lauryn Hamilton's horse rescue is sure to benefit. But rodeo star Gavin Kingsley has his devilish, bad boy gaze on *her*. The good girl. The one who's never ruled by reckless passion—until now...

#2926 THE INHERITANCE TEST

by Anne Marsh

Movie star Declan Masterson needs to rehabilitate his playboy image fast to save his inheritance! Partnering with Jane Charlotte—the quintessential "plain jane"—for a charity yacht race is a genius first step. If only there wasn't a captivating woman underneath Jane's straightlaced exterior...

#2927 BILLIONAIRE FAKE OUT

The Image Project • by Katherine Garbera

Paisley Campbell just learned her lover is a famous Hollywood A-lister... and she's expecting his baby! Sean O'Neill knows he's been living on borrowed time by keeping his identity secret. Can he convince her that everything they shared was not just a celebrity stunt?

#2928 A GAME OF SECRETS

The Eddington Heirs • by Zuri Day

CEO Jake Eddington was charged with protecting his friend's beautiful sister from players and users. And he knows *he* should resist their chemistry too...but socialite Sasha McDowell is too captivating to ignore—even if their tryst ignites a scandal...

HDCNM1222

HARLEQUIN
PLUS

Announcing a **BRAND-NEW**
multimedia subscription service
for romance fans like you!

Read, Watch and Play.

Experience the easiest way to get
the romance content you crave.

Start your **FREE 7 DAY TRIAL** at
<u>www.harlequinplus.com/freetrial</u>.